SPIRIT WALKER

The Hunting of Man

Book Two of Dead or Alive: Mason Hill Series

Written by Michael Kidwell

Spirit Walker

The Serpent... 4

The Hunting of Man...20

The Wicked..45

The Return of Coyote.................................... 49

Aftermath.. 51

False Profit...54

The Spirit Walker and Coyote...................... 62

Deadly Mistake.. 75

The Warriors Morning Bird and Meniish.....84

Mason and Gabriella.....................................96

The Beast Awakens.......................................107

Evil Lurks...111

Flight of The Ghost.......................................114

Closing In.. 118

Death Sentence... 124

The Reckoning...126

The Serpent

Marshall Delbert Crenshaw peered through the red sun-bleached curtains of his dark hotel room. Across the dusty road from the ramshackle hotel was the Lucky Shoe Saloon, and inside, destroying his liver, was Ervin Wells, a six-foot-seven-inch slender man with stringy black hair, pointed features, and the narrow eyes of a serpent. He was a cold-blooded killer with no friends and loved solely by his mother.

Ervin had been on the run for three months after escaping an unlocked sheriff's transport wagon outside Big Rock City, Oklahoma.

He managed to strangle both deputies with his wrist shackles. Then calmly took their guns, ammunition, and horses and fled, but not before leaving his calling card, an X carved on both the deputies' foreheads.

To describe Ervin as a run-of-the-mill criminal would be an understatement. He was convicted of murdering six people, spanning the entire state of Oklahoma.

Murder was the driving force of Ervin's existence, and his lust for it was insatiable, followed secondly by occasional robbery.

No one knew how many men, women, and children Ervin had killed, but he did. Each murder, down to the last detail, was branded into his mind and carefully shelved in his macabre mental library.

Ervin relished every memory, often revisiting his favorites when he needed to appease his desire to kill.

What troubled Delbert was knowing Ervin would hang, having been charged with the killings of six but suspected of killing dozens more. But, in the end, it didn't matter; Ervin would die regardless of whether it was six or six hundred, and Delbert would be there to witness the last breath Ervin took on this earth.

Delbert recalled a brief conversation he had three years earlier with a murdering thief named Josie Peche. Before the bottom fell out of the hangman's platform, Peche looked him straight in the eyes and grinned before saying, "Well, Marshall, I guess this is goodbye. Enjoy the moment. You can only kill me once."

Peche's words stuck with Delbert, and the point was well taken. You can't hang a man separately for every crime he's committed. It's a one-time deal, all cards in.

Delbert leaned back in the wobbly chair. It squeaked and cracked, protesting the position it was forced to take and never designed for.

It was late. Delbert began feeling the overwhelming need for sleep. He glanced over his shoulder at the dank bed behind him. In any other circumstance, he would have been disgusted, but sitting in the dark, serenaded by the muffled sound of the saloon's piano, the bed with its flat pillow and crumpled blanket which someone had carelessly thrown on the heavily stained mattress looked strangely welcoming.

That was the last thing Delbert remembered before waking with his chin resting on his chest. Outside, the morning gray had already begun turning yellow as the sun crept from behind the mountains in the east.

Delbert rocked forward frantically, pulling the curtains aside. Across the street, the saloon was quiet. The boardwalk that had been crowded with boisterous drunks and gamblers the night before was abandoned. Replaced by a young man who busied himself scraping plastered cow manure from the steps leading into the front doors of the Lucky Shoe.

A large wagon loaded with lumber clattered up the street, blocking Delbert's view of the young man.

As the wagon passed, Delbert watched the driver; as he held the reins and fumbled with the collar of his coat, buttoning it to ward off the creeping cold of the morning.

With an uninterested wave at the wagon driver, the boy turned and walked inside the Lucky Shoe.

Delbert hurriedly stepped past the bed. Then, with a last glance at the room, he shouldered his rifle and walked out of the hotel and into the brisk morning air.

Delbert missed his target. Ervin was gone, and the likelihood of him being in town was slim. As Delbert walked toward the Livery, he questioned his ability to continue working as a U.S. Marshall.

Delbert was fifty-five years old, and as he got older, the criminals got younger; Delbert was feeling the effects of age; he couldn't recall a time when he had fallen asleep when he had a wanted man in sight, especially one as dangerous as Ervin Wells.

Fortunately, Delbert had yet to send a telegram to the U.S. Marshall's office stating he was in Ribbon Wood or that he had located Wells. Explaining he had lost Wells would not have sat well with the upper command.

Rumors regarding Delbert's age and efficiency were already circulating; this latest gaffe would likely have been the death knell of a long and, up until lately, a very successful career.

As Delbert walked past the Ribbon Wood post office, he noticed an overweight red-headed postman sitting at his desk, sifting through a pile of envelopes. Delbert glanced at the open sign hanging on the door; still, he respectfully tapped on the door before opening it, startling the chubby man.

The Postman spastically stood from his chair, looking like a child caught with his hand in a cookie jar.

The Postman nervously cleared his throat, eyeing Delbert's rifle warily.

"Good morning, sir, or should I say good day?" He faltered. "What I mean is, how are you?"

Delbert waved his hand.

"Good morning is fine. Could you do me a favor and send a telegram?"

The Postman nervously wiped his sweating palms on the sides of his wrinkled vest.

"I can, but the Post Office isn't open for another hour."

Delbert thumbed over his shoulder. "The sign on the door says you're open."

The Postman fidgeted nervously.

"Give me a second."

The Postman immediately sifted through the envelopes before realizing the stub of a pencil he was looking for was behind his ear. With a shaky hand, he held the pencil towards Delbert.

" Write what you want to be sent and where."

Delbert had a feeling that the Postman had been up to more than just sorting mail. Delbert grinned; the Postman was probably a twisted little man who enjoyed reading others' mail. Or worse, he was a mail thief. Either way, it didn't matter.

Delbert took the pencil and a small square of paper from the desk.

"The telegram is going to the Post Office in Laudry and addressed to a friend of mine named Two Dogs."

The Postman wrinkled his nose. "Two Dogs, what the hell kind of name is Two Dogs?"

Delbert glared at the Postman. "Two Dogs is my partner and the best Tracker alive."

The Postman's face blazed red. "I'm sorry, sir; I didn't mean nothing by it."

Delbert ignored the man and continued writing his message.

When he finished, Delbert eyed the Postman. "Here you are, sir; I'll wait until you send it."

The Postman quickly took Delbert's note before sitting in front of the telegraph machine.

As Delbert waited, he idly scanned a wall covered with public notices when he spotted the corner of a wanted poster sticking out from behind a stack of curled and tattered papers.

The wanted poster had a large sketch of a young man named Mason Hill.

Delbert ripped the sign from the wall, ignoring the rest of the papers as they fell to the floor.

The Postman looked up from the telegraph machine, "Is something wrong, Mr.?"

Delbert furiously waved the wanted poster.

"What the hell is this?"

The Postman nervously licked his dry lips, "It's a wanted poster, Mr. Haven't you ever seen one before?"

Delbert turned his back on the Postman, searching for the declaration of pardon that should have been hung in place of the wanted poster.

There was no declaration of pardon. Delbert turned, facing the Postman.

"Where the hell is the declaration of pardon for this man? He isn't wanted."

The Postman glanced anxiously across the street toward the Sheriff's Office.

"Mr., I don't know anything about that. You'd have to talk to the Sheriff. He's the one who puts the wanted posters up, not me."

Delbert paid the Postman, slamming the door behind him as he left.

The postman rushed to the door, hastily flipping the sign from open to closed before locking it and returning to his desk. After glancing at the locked door, the Postman picked up a heavily perfumed letter and resumed sniffing it as he had been before he was interrupted.

Delbert stomped through the unlocked door of the Sheriff's Office.

A thin old man with a bushy gray mustache calmly peered over the top of his cup of coffee. The old man sipped his charcoal black coffee before setting his chipped mug on his desk.

Delbert eyed the man, if not for a battered badge dangling loosely from the old man's shirt. Delbert would never have assumed he was a Lawman.

The Sheriff regarded Delbert with disinterested rheumy eyes.

"Sir, before you come any closer, I'm going to have to ask you to put that rifle down."

Delbert leaned his rifle beside the door before removing his hat. Angry or not, Delbert would not treat the old man disrespectfully in his office.

"Are you the Sheriff?"

The old man leaned forward in his chair. Delbert recognized the old man's repositioning as that of an experienced Lawman. Leaning forward exposed less of his center mass, which would otherwise have been an easy target for even the poorest shooter. He also rightly assumed the Sheriff had a shotgun wired under the desk.

The old man grinned; he had seen more than one hot-headed drunk burst through his door and thought Delbert was another.

"That's what the badge says. What can I do for you?"

Delbert sat in a wobbly chair in front of the battered desk.

"The name is Marshall Crenshaw." Delbert slid the wanted poster across the Sheriff's desk. "I came here because of this."

The Sheriff glanced from the poster to Delbert. "Did you find this young fella?"

Delbert impatiently tapped his knee. "Sheriff, that man isn't wanted. He was pardoned."

The Sheriff opened his desk drawer, pulling out a large tattered binder. Without explaining what he was doing, he flipped through wanted posters, stopping at a declaration of pardon with the name and sketch of Mason Hill.

The Sheriff glanced at the wanted poster before lingering over the declaration of pardon. Then, finally, he looked up at Delbert.

"Well, sure enough, that kid has a full pardon."

Delbert felt anger welling. "Yes, he does. Do you want to explain why you still have that wanted poster in the Post Office? The U.S. Marshalls Office sent the pardon declaration out for a reason."

The Sheriff closed the binder. "Not that I need to explain anything to you, but I'll be honest. My mind isn't what it used to be. I remember the pardon. I simply forgot to hang it up. I've got no other excuse."

Delbert sighed; the old man was honest. He made no excuses; for that, he had his respect.

Delbert stood from the chair, extending his right hand to the Sheriff. The old Sheriff stood, shaking Delbert's hand.

"I'll hang the pardon. The name is Lucas Greene, Sheriff Lucas Greene."

Delbert nodded, "Nice to meet you, Sheriff."

"Marshall, I'm curious before you head out. Did you come here just to check on wanted posters?"

Delbert picked up his rifle. "No sir, I have other business. I have a U.S. Government Tracker coming into town tomorrow. Odds are, when he gets here, we'll be leaving."

Greene scratched his head. "A tracker; you must have someone you're really interested in catching."

Delbert grinned; the Sheriff had no idea just how interested he was in catching Ervin.

"The man I'm looking for is smart as a fox, and he doesn't stay in the same place for long. That's why I need a tracker."

Delbert opened the door.

"Marshall, just curious. Who is this tracker?"

Debert glanced over his shoulder. "His name is Two Dogs."

Greene opened his mouth to speak, but the words wouldn't come.

Delbert closed the door. "Sheriff, you look like you've seen a ghost."

Greene slowly sat in his chair. "Marshall, I know Two Dogs."

Delbert walked across the room to the desk. "You know Two Dogs, how?"

Greene stood from his chair. Then, without saying a word, he walked to the front window of the office, staring at the vacant road.

"Marshall, before they elected me Sheriff of this godforsaken town, I was a Captain in the U.S. Calvary. I was the man responsible for capturing Two Dogs and his warriors. I'm the man who put the noose around the necks of all of them." Greene turned, facing Delbert, "I made Two Dogs watch while we hung every one of his warriors. It's not something I'm proud of, and if I could take it back, I would, but I had orders."

Delbert nodded. "Sheriff, that was over ten years ago. I would have done the same thing. The thing is, Two Dogs has more than repaid his debt. He's tracked down and hauled in more criminals than most Lawmen will in their entire careers."

Greene returned to his chair. "I'm sure he has." Greene cleared his throat. "Marshall, my detachment did more than hang Two Dogs' warriors. We massacred an entire Apache village. Men, women, and children, they weren't Two Dogs people. Those people had nothing to do with causing any problems; they were just living their lives. But that didn't matter. We had orders to kill or capture any Apaches we came across, so we did. I don't know if Two Dogs knows that I led those men, but do me a favor when he gets here. Let him know I'm sorry."

Delbert nodded before stepping out the door. "I'll let him know."

Several doors down from the Sheriff's Office, the unmistakable sound of a single gunshot blasted from inside the Sheriff's Office.

Delbert glanced over his shoulder, whispering under his breath.

"God forgive you, Sheriff."

Delbert spent the remainder of the day walking the streets of Ribbon Wood. The town was a busy boom town filled with people from all walks of life with one thing in common: gold.

While only a few struck it rich, the other hopefuls were able to scratch a meager living from the ground and the bottom of gravel river bottoms, but the days of striking it rich had long passed.

Most of the buildings lining Main Street were well-constructed. They housed a wide variety of shops, restaurants, and specialty stores. In contrast, others were hastily constructed and roofed with canvas.

Those were built by newcomers eager to cash in on the rumored bounty of riches hoarded by successful prospectors.

What the newcomers didn't know was that ten years of mining had virtually tapped out the once plentiful gold supply. Even so, many silver-tongued land brokers and claim owners sold stripped mines and fruitless parcels of land at exorbitant prices. For them, there was still money to be made in Ribbon Wood.

* * *

After searching every saloon and hotel in town, it was clear that either no one had seen Ervin or was interested in providing any information. The only tiny bit of information came from a filthy town drunk named Dunkin Brown, and the information he provided came with the cost of a bottle of cheap whiskey.

Brown claimed he had seen a stranger at an abandoned farmhouse south of town. Brown explained that the stranger was using the house as a hideout.

When Delbert told Brown Ervin's name, he shrugged as he glanced longingly at a saloon across the road. That's when the price for further information was negotiated, resulting in the purchase of the bottle of whiskey.

Once Delbert paid for the bottle, Brown uncorked it, gulping down three mouthfuls. Then, with a wink and a staggering bump against Delbert's shoulder, Brown grinned.

"I'm not sure if the man's name was Ervin or Ernest; all I know is it started with an E."

It wasn't much, but it was all Delbert had.

Delbert settled into his room at the Lucky Strike Hotel early that evening. It was a decent place near the train station, boasting clean rooms and beds.

True to the owner's advertisement, the rooms were clean, and the beds were neatly made with laundered bedding, a much-appreciated upgrade from the squalor of the Gold Strike Hotel, where he spent the night before.

Delbert woke early to the sound of a train horn. From his room, he could see the station, and to no surprise, his partner and closest friend, Two Dogs, was the last to disembark.

Two Dogs was a middle-aged man who undoubtedly was Apache. While on assignment, he wore his approved government clothing, a brown riding coat, blue shirt, and tan pants.

The Marshalls Office compromised and allowed Two Dogs to keep his long hair, which he kept pulled back and neatly braided. Even so, there was no doubt in anyone's mind who saw him that Two Dogs was a fearsome warrior.

Delbert watched in amusement as mothers pulled their children closer and men stepped aside as Two Dogs made his way to the livery car. If they knew him like Delbert, they would know Two Dogs was a loyal, friendly man who treated ordinary people with respect. However, if you were unfortunate enough to be of interest to the

Marshalls Office, Two Dogs was a relentless hunter of man who would stop at nothing to track you down and bring you to justice.

Delbert stepped to his old friend's side as Two Dogs saddled his horse.

"Well, my old friend, I'm glad to see you."

Two Dogs turned, grinning at his friend. "I'm glad to see you; it s been six months, too long not to see you, Delbert."

As he shook his old friend's hand, Delbert realized how much he missed Two Dogs.

"Dogs, I wish we could stick around and see the sites, but we have a serious problem. I lost Ervin. I had him, Dogs; he was in a saloon across the street from my hotel room, and I lost him."

"How did you lose him? You're telegraph said you were close to catching him. You said nothing about losing him."

Delbert was ashamed, but he wouldn't lie to Two Dogs.

"I fell asleep, Dogs, simple as that, I just fell asleep, and he got away."

Two Dogs grinned, "Delbert, we are getting too old for this job."

"I know Dogs. I've been thinking about that for a while now, and rumor has it so has the Marshall's Office. The thing is, I don't know what I'd do with myself if I were retired."

"I've told you before, Delbert; you can live with me and my people. You would be safe there. Maybe even settle down and have a wife. They have heard many stories about you; my people would be honored to have you live with them."

Delbert patted Two Dogs' shoulder. "I know Dogs, and I've told you, you can live with me. We could buy some land and do some ranching."

"I know what you have told me." Two Dogs shrugged. "For now, we have many years left in us. We will keep this up as long as possible, then talk about other things."

"Agreed; by the way, Two Dogs, did you know a man named Lucas Greene?"

Two Dogs' eyes narrowed. "I knew a man with that name; he was a Cavalry Captain. I will kill him for what he did to my warriors and to innocent Apache; he is a killer."

Delbert nodded. "Dogs, I talked to him; he wanted you to know he was sorry for what he did."

Two Dogs smirked. "I do not accept his apology. Unfortunately, Greene's debt can only be paid with his life."

"Dogs, he's dead. I talked to him yesterday. He was the Sheriff. He told me to tell you he was sorry for what he did. When I left his Office, he shot himself."

Two Dogs spat. "He took a coward's path. He knew I would kill him."

"Maybe so, Dogs, but the fact is he's dead."

Two Dogs returned his attention to his horse, checking his saddle.

"I'm happy he is dead. When I return to my people, I will let them know he cheated us by taking his own life."

Delbert nodded. There was nothing more he could say on the matter.

Two Dogs mounted his horse. "When do we leave?"

"Now, Ervin has a day lead on us."

Within an hour, Two Dogs spotted a single trail of horse prints leading away from the road in a southerly direction.

Two Dogs examined the hoof prints. His years of experience and impossibly accurate intuition prompted him to follow the trail.

"Delbert, these are his tracks; he left the road to avoid attention."

Delbert knew there was no doubt that the tracks were Ervin's. What perplexed him was why Ervin would leave the road to avoid attention.

Dogs, I'm not questioning you, but Ervin didn't seem to have a problem sitting in a busy saloon. I don't know why he would worry about being seen on his way out of town."

Two Dogs nodded Southwest. "I do not know why he left the road, but he did. He is heading this way."

Delbert grinned; he reconsidered the story Brown had told him; maybe there was some truth to it.

"Lead the way, Dogs.

The Hunting of Man

Delbert lay on his stomach, peering at the small crumbling farmhouse. The house appeared uninhabited if not for a thin ribbon of smoke trailing from the chimney.

Tattered curtains fluttered lazily from the glassless window frames. The roof that once sheltered the home now buckled and heaved from countless years of weathering and disrepair. The small porch, once used as a place to enjoy summer evenings, was now a splintered skeleton of what it once had been.

A frayed rope remained hanging from the branch of a large oak tree in the front yard, testimony that children once played there, but now the children, along with their family, were gone, taking with them the memories of family life and childhood adventures spent long ago.

Long ago, a loving family once inhabited what was left of the proud little house; but now it housed a sadistic killer who, like a roach, lurked within its four walls, contaminating everything he touched.

Delbert glanced at Two Dogs, who had positioned himself at the corner of the precariously leaning barn. Two Dogs knelt on his knee; his rifle trained steadily at the house.

Seeing no movement from within the house, Delbert ran to the oak tree before aiming at the window beside the door. He waited and listened for any sound from within, but all was silent.

Delbert glanced anxiously toward Two Dogs. Something wasn't right. Ervin supposedly used the house as a temporary hideout, but his horse was nowhere to be seen, and the house was too quiet. All the same, there was the smoking chimney. Someone was inside or had recently been there.

Two Dogs crept from the corner of the barn, crouching as he made his way to the west side of the house.

Delbert watched as Two Dogs cautiously separated the curtains with the barrel of his rifle.

Peering inside, Two Dogs discovered the house was empty, except for a raccoon that startled at the sight of him. In desperation to hide, the raccoon ran across the top of a makeshift table, knocking a warped plate to the littered floor.

Two Dogs glanced at the fireplace; the coals smoldered, evident that whoever had made the fire had left hours ago.

Still erring on the side of caution, Two Dogs crept onto the porch, keeping his rifle trained on the front window.

As Two Dogs placed his hand on the doorknob, he glanced at Delbert, who was still covering him from behind the oak tree.

Delbert nodded. He knew his old friend well and knew Two Dogs wouldn't open the door until he was certain Delbert was ready.

Seeing Delbert nod, Two Dogs turned the doorknob before kicking the door open.

Two Dogs quickly entered the house, followed closely by Delbert. Each man aimed their rifle opposite the other as they continued forward. Once they reached the opposite side of the house, they lowered their guns. The house was empty.

Two Dogs opened the back door, glancing at the left and right corners of the house.

"He is not here."

Delbert shouldered his rifle. "He's a slick one, Dogs. I'll bet he got wind of us being in the area."

Two Dogs shrugged, "This man is a ghost."

Delbert knelt before the fireplace, examining the patterns in the dust.

"He slept here last night. I guess the cold got to him, so he made a fire and curled up right here in front of it."

Two Dogs nodded before pinching a half-smoked cigar from the splintered table. He rolled the chewed end between his fingers.

"It's still wet."

Delbert stood, eyeing the cigar.

"Looks like Ervin felt right at home and figured he'd have a smoke before he set out."

Two Dogs flicked the cigar into the coals before glancing into the shadows of a doorless bedroom. Like the rest of the house, it was littered with leaves that blew through the shattered windows and trash left behind by passing travelers, but something else caught his attention.

Delbert turned his attention from the fireplace to Two Dogs.

Two Dogs knelt as he took aim at something in the bedroom. Delbert slowly stood, aiming his rifle in the same direction.

Delbert followed Two Dogs into the filthy bedroom. The shredded curtains fluttered inward, carrying an icy wind behind them. A rusted can fell from the windowsill, clanging onto the floor before rolling across the room.

Two Dogs stepped closer to a pile of tattered clothes in the closet when he noticed a small stocking-covered foot protruding from the pile. Two Dogs carefully used the end of his rifle to toss the pile of rags from the body beneath.

It was a young blond-haired woman. A length of frayed rope wrapped around her neck revealed the method of her execution, and the X carved into her forehead left no doubt about who had committed the act.

Delbert lowered his rifle. "Damn, that son of a bitch. She isn't more than sixteen or seventeen years old."

Two Dogs covered the young girl's face. "Age doesn't matter to the Ghost. He kills because it brings him joy. This is why he left the road. She did not come here willingly; he took her."

Delbert stepped out of the room in disgust, returning to the fireplace.

Two Dogs followed, "What do we do? If we go back to town, it will set us back many hours."

Delbert shrugged, "We have no choice, Dogs; we can't leave her here like this. She has a family, friends, maybe a husband."

Two Dogs knew Delbert wouldn't leave the young woman's body behind especially considering how close town was.

After a moment of thinking, Two Dogs agreed with Delbert. If the young woman had a family, they should know what had happened to her.

"Well, Dogs, how about you get a fire going? I'll ride back to town and have a wagon come out here for the girl."

Two Dogs shrugged. "I'll leave the girl where she is. I'm going to ride out and find Ervin's trail."

Delbert glanced outside at the heavy snow-laden clouds, "I'll be back as quick as I can." Delbert hesitated, "Dogs depending on the weather, we might have to stay here for the night."

Two Dogs stepped past Delbert, squinting as he looked up at the clouds. "We will stay here. We will freeze if we get caught in the snow."

Delbert smirked. "If we're lucky, Ervin will freeze to death.

* * *

Ervin's trail was easy to find. Two Dogs followed the faint impressions left behind by Ervin's horse as they traveled west.

After following the tracks for an hour, the snow began falling, first in light flurries, then in white sheets, cutting visibility to mere feet.

Two Dogs knew there was no need to continue and risk becoming lost in a snowstorm. With a final glance at the disappearing hoof prints, he turned his horse, nudging it back to the dilapidated house. Upon Two Dogs' return, a wagon with two men and a coffin were leaving the property's front yard.

Two Dogs rode into the barn where Delbert busied himself, covering his horse with a blanket.

Hearing Two Dogs horse behind him, Delbert glanced over his shoulder.

"The acting Sheriff said he recognized the girl. She's new to these parts and just started working at the White Orchid Saloon."

Two Dogs tethered his horse beside Delbert's. "Does she have a family?"

Delbert shrugged, "Doesn't look like it, not in these parts anyway. The Sheriff said he's going to ask around if anyone saw anything strange last night."

Two Dogs nodded, "It doesn't matter; we already know who did it."

"That's what I told the Sheriff, but he still has a job to do. If he doesn't ask questions, he may find his new position short-lived."

Delbert stepped past Two Dogs toward a pile of dusty firewood. "Did you find Ervin's trail?"

Two Dogs nodded. "He is heading west, but he won't travel far in this." Two Dogs glanced toward the house. "The snow might be a problem. It will cover his trail."

Delbert shrugged. "I have faith in you, Dogs; you'll find Ervin's trail."

Two Dogs knew he would find Ervin's trail; it would simply take him a little longer to do so. Two Dogs knelt beside the barn entrance, gathering an armful of the firewood before following Delbert into the house.

Once Delbert and Two Dogs had built a small fire, they gathered the remnants of the tattered clothing scattered throughout the house and covered the gaping windows. It wasn't much, but it cut down the icy wind that seeped into the house.

Neither man cared for the idea of sleeping in the same spot Ervin had the night before, but it was the warmest place in the house.

As Delbert sat beside Two Dogs, he tossed a log onto the fire.

"I'll bet that son of a bitch killed that girl right where we're sitting."

Two Dogs glanced around the room. "The Ghost kills wherever he feels like killing. He is not human. For most, killing someone is done for a reason, not pleasure. The Ghost kills because he likes to."

Delbert glanced at Two Dogs. He knew Two Dogs and his warriors had killed scores of people. Some of which Debert was sure they killed for no other reason than they could. All the same, what Two Dogs said was true; Ervin loved killing.

As if Two Dogs knew what his friend was thinking, he looked into Delbert's eyes.

"I never killed for pleasure. I killed to protect my people's land from intruders, but they kept coming. They were like trails of ants, and like ants, they were unstoppable."

Two Dogs' words were true; settlers recklessly plundered the land that once belonged to the Apache, and they did so with a sense of impunity, often killing the Apache with no concerns of legal repercussions, as there were none.

Outside, the wind howled, causing the house to creak like a battered ship at sea. Delbert looked up at the rafters as a rat ran along the crossbeam.

The place was filthy, but he was thankful for it. Delbert imagined a time long ago when the house would have been clean and warm and filled with laughter and the simple conversations of a happy family.

The fireplace he and Two Dogs huddled in front of would have been the focal point for the family on nights such as this. Stories would have been told to the children as they lay in front of a warm fire, followed by a tuck into bed by their parents.

Now the fireplace was the site where a psychopath had killed and slept, and where the law would sleep the following night, and once gone, rodents and other vermin would reclaim their castle.

Delbert contemplated burning the place to the ground when they left but decided not to. Although the wild rodents of the land were not welcome in an occupied home, this house would never be lived in by humans again. It had become the home of vermin, and Delbert didn't see the sense in taking that away from them.

Two Dogs walked through the house, peering out the windows for any sign of Ervin. There wasn't much to be seen other than the shadow of the barn shrouded by the driving snow.

Two Dogs returned to his spot, covering himself in his bedroll.

"If the Ghost is out there, he won't live for long."

Delbert grinned, "Well, I hope he is out there, and I hope he doesn't live for long."

Two Dogs lay back, closing his eyes. "He won't."

* * *

The two men woke early. The blowing snow had stopped sometime during the night, leaving behind a powdery landscape in its wake.

As Delbert and Two Dogs rode from the barn, they snugly wrapped their scarves around their faces. It did little to cut the cold but it was better than nothing.

As the two men left the yard, Delbert glanced over his shoulder at the house. It may have been home to rodents, but the smoke swirling from its chimney promised a reprieve from the freezing temperature outside and temporary warmth for the raccoon and rodents within; Delbert was glad he hadn't burned the place to the ground.

The sun began breaking through the clouds several miles from the house, providing brief periods of relief from the frigid air.

After several hours of riding, Two Dogs halted his horse and pointed to a dense growth of pine in the distance.

"That's where I would go if I had to sleep out here."

Delbert eyed the trees. "So would I. What's your plan? We're in the wide open."

Two Dogs pulled his rifle from its sheath, laying it across his lap.

"I think we should act as if we are hunting. If the Ghost is in there, he's already seen us."

Delbert glanced at Two Dogs. "So you think we should just ride on towards those trees like we don't have a care in the world?"

Two Dogs smiled. He knew Delbert didn't like the idea. "Yes, like we are hunting deer."

Delbert frowned; he felt Two Dogs' plan bordered on recklessness.

"Well, I sure hope Ervin can't shoot. We'll be sitting ducks."

Two Dogs nudged his horse towards the trees. "He only kills with his hands. I don't think he is good with a gun."

"I don't think that's why he kills with his hands. I think he does it because he likes to watch the people he's killing die."

Two Dogs continued casually riding towards the trees.

"Maybe, or maybe he can't shoot."

Delbert grinned. He knew Two Dogs all too well. If Two Dogs thought Ervin couldn't shoot, then that's how it would stand until proven otherwise.

They didn't have to search long before Two Dogs spotted a makeshift shelter made of branches and pine boughs.

Two Dogs was impressed. Ervin had done quite well constructing his temporary home, including banking his fire inside the structure for warmth.

As Two Dogs examined Ervin's camp, he discovered tracks leading from the campsite revealing Ervin had left hours earlier. Unmelted snow dotting the coals further confirmed Two Dogs' suspicion.

Without a word, Two Dogs continued forward, following Ervin's trail. As Two Dogs expected, the path led from the trees and continued west across the snow-covered grasslands.

Delbert rode alongside Two Dogs. "If I were a betting man, I would say that Ervin is heading for Geyser Springs."

Two Dogs glanced at Delbert. "What's in Geyser Springs?"

"A lot, It's a big town with a train station. People from all over are coming and going there."

Two Dogs sighed. "If the Ghost gets on a train, it will be like it was when Mason led us everywhere."

Delbert nodded. "I was thinking the same thing. I just hope he's not as smart as Mason."

Two Dogs shrugged. "No man is as smart as Mason."

Ervin's trail eventually dissolved into the muddy road leading into Geyser Springs, blending with a myriad of wagon and horse tracks.

As Delbert and Two Dogs rode into the busy town, they noticed the weather didn't appear to have affected commerce.

Wagons creaked, bumped, and splashed up and down the main street at a clip, which Delbert and Two Dogs considered dangerous.

The boardwalk and stores lining both sides of the main road bustled with people from all walks of life, and no one seemed interested in what anyone else was doing.

Two Dogs remained silent as he scanned the many faces of Geyser Springs. He didn't expect to see Ervin among the crowd, nevertheless, he wasn't about to let Ervin slip past him.

Delbert glanced over his shoulder toward Two Dogs. "Are you okay, Dogs?"

Two Dogs nodded. "I don't like this place. There are too many people."

Delbert grinned. "I feel the same. I don't know how anyone could live like this. I'll take the wide open country over this any day."

Delbert spotted the train station as they continued toward the center of town.

"Before we busy ourselves searching this town, let's check the station and see if Ervin bought a ticket."

Delbert and Two Dogs snaked their horses up the chaotic street before reaching the station. When they reached the ticket counter, Delbert slid the wanted poster toward the railway operator.

Without a word, the old bearded man sitting behind the counter removed his glasses from his vest pocket and squinted at the poster. He glanced up at Delbert and Two Dogs before further examining the poster.

"I recall seeing this young fellow about three hours ago or so, bought himself a ticket to Kingman, Arizona. He said something about doing some hunting down that way."

Delbert glanced at Two Dogs. They both knew what kind of hunting Ervin planned on doing.

Delbert tapped nervously on the counter. "Did he take his horse?"

The old man grinned, exposing the only yellow tooth he had left.

"He sure did. Had it put on the livestock car."

The old man handed Delbert the poster. "If you're looking to catch the next train to Kingman, you'll have to wait until eight thirty tomorrow morning."

Although frustrated, Delbert nodded. There was no point in hassling the old man about the train schedule. There was nothing the old man could do about it.

"Well then, I guess we'll have to wait until then."

The old man pulled out two pieces of paper from the drawer in front of him.

"If you buy your tickets now, I'll stamp them for you. Alongside the station is a restaurant with a hotel. It's clean, with decent rooms above it. The lady who runs the place gives a little discount to ticket holders."

Delbert and Two Dogs had planned to buy their train tickets anyway. So a discount for room and board was a welcome break in the deal.

After boarding their horses, they entered the restaurant. The old man was right. The restaurant below the hotel was clean and brightly lit, and the food was much better than a fistful of beef jerky.

The plump red-cheeked German woman who owned the place honored the promised discount and rented two rooms to Delber and Two Dogs.

Although it was early, neither man wanted to roam the streets. As Two Dogs put it, "There were too many people with too many problems out there."

After supper, Delbert and Two Dogs sat on a large sofa in front of the restaurant's stone fireplace.

The German woman offered them whiskey, but neither of them was interested in drinking anything other than coffee.

The German woman smiled as she returned with their coffee, taking particular interest in Delbert.

"If you're interested, my name is Ella."

Delbert felt Two Dogs gently elbow him.

Delbert smiled politely. "Well, Ella, it's nice to meet you, I'm Marshall Delbert Crenshaw, and this is Tracker Two Dogs."

Ella stared at Delbert, grinning like she had never seen a man before.

"Marshall, I like Lawmen, and I like them more when they don't drink. I serve the poison but only because travelers ask for it."

Delbert knew Ella had mistaken his not drinking as him being a Christian man, which he considered himself to be, but only when it suited him.

"That's real nice, Ella, but I do drink on occasion, but tonight coffee sounded better."

Ella was unfazed by Delbert's admission of immorality.

"That's okay, Marshall; a man can have a nip now and again; that doesn't make him a sinner."

Much to Delbert's disappointment, Two Dogs stood.

"Delbert, I need sleep. Ella, it was nice to meet you. Delbert, tell Ella about the time we tracked down the Toller brothers. It is a good story."

Two Dogs winked before stepping upstairs, leaving Delbert to the mercy of Ella.

As Two Dogs opened the door to his room, he heard Ella speaking as sweet as honey to Delbert.

"Marshall, no one is here tonight. I'm closing so we can sit together. I want to hear all your stories."

* * *

Two Dogs grinned at Delbert the following morning as they boarded the train for Kingman.

"Delbert, I heard many strange noises last night. I was afraid Ella was hurting you."

Delbert removed his hat before running his fingers through his hair.

"You're not funny, Two Dogs; you left me down there alone with her, and yes, she did hurt me. She tossed me all over her bedroom like I was a ragdoll. I'm too old for all that."

Two Dogs shrugged. "Delbert, are you limping?"

Delbert ignored Two Dogs as he scanned the train car for a seat.

Eventually, Two Dogs and Delbert sat at the rear of the train. A solid wall behind them suited them more than exposing their backs to strangers.

More than one Lawman had met his end in a train car by an assassin seated directly behind him, but that wasn't going to be the case with either one of them.

As Delbert and Two Dogs sat side by side, they scanned the train car for anyone who looked familiar or could pose a threat. Fortunately, no one looked or acted suspicious. However, as they relaxed, two Marshalls entered the car with a shackled young man between them.

Delbert and Two Dogs instantly recognized one of the Marshalls by his immense size. It was Tommy Gorge, and the shorter

Marshall was Levi Timmins. Both Marshalls had ridden with Delbert and Two Dogs for over a year while they futilely hunted a then-wanted criminal named Mason Hill.

Tommy grinned when he spotted Delbert and Two Dogs seated at the back of the train. Tommy glanced over the head of the shackled young man toward Levi.

"Levi, look who's here."

Levi struggled to see who Tommy was talking about, but Tommy's colossal frame blocked his view.

"Goddamn it, Tommy, I can't see anything around that big melon head of yours."

Tommy ignored Levi. "Well, I'll be darned if it isn't Marshall Delbert Crenshaw and Tracker Two Dogs."

Tommy shuffled towards the men, dragging the young man and Levi behind him.

Delbert and Two Dogs stood before shaking Tommy and Levi's hands.

"Well, aren't you two a sight for sore eyes? I heard about you two catching up with that Mason Hill kid." Levi grinned. "Heard he got himself all shot to hell and died."

Two Dogs nodded. "Mason was shot, but not by us. When we left him, he was with his pregnant wife and family, but he wasn't dead. I hope he survived. He is a good man."

Tommy maneuvered his massive frame into his seat near the window, dragging the shackled young man into the middle seat.

"I hope he survived, too. He was an innocent man," said Tommy.

Levi agreed, "We had some good times looking for that Mason, but we wasted a long time hunting that poor kid for nothing. It almost cost us our jobs."

The shackled young man glanced from Tommy to Levi. "Sounds like me. I'm an innocent man accused of a murder I had nothing to do with."

Delbert nodded toward the young man. "So what's his story?"

Levi glanced at Delbert as he inspected the shackles and locks on the young man's wrists and ankles.

"This here is Darcy Boone; he shot and killed a barkeep in Montana before running off and killing a card dealer in Idaho, and for his final act, he shot and killed a Sunday school teacher in Wyoming." Levi flicked the side of Darcy's head, causing him to flinch. "Make no mistake, we got the right man, and we're on our way to Kingman, where he'll be tried and hanged."

Delbert's brow furrowed. "Why Kingman? That's nowhere near where he killed those people."

Levi shrugged. "The Mayor and some other elected officials of Kingman are trying to pass all sorts of laws and ordinances. To do that, they need convictions to support their proposed laws. It doesn't matter if the crimes were committed there or not, so long as the accused is tried and convicted in their jurisdiction, they can claim the stats."

"Something isn't right about doing things that way," said Two Dogs.

Tommy nodded, "Agreed, Two Dogs, but our orders were to find this kid and deliver him to the authorities in Kingman. We don't get involved in the politics of judicial officials."

The train's steam horn blared, and its bell rang as it heaved forward. The journey to Kingman had begun.

Tommy continued, "So what do they have you two doing? You're a long way from home."

Delbert leaned forward. "We're searching for a killer by the name of Ervin Wells. I almost had him in Ribbon Wood, but he ducked out before I could catch him. Anyway, he's heading to Kingman, then only God knows where unless Dogs and I catch him."

Upon hearing Ervin's name, Tommy's eyes widened, as did Levi's.

Levi glanced to his left, where a mother and three children were seated. Fortunately, they appeared uninterested in their conversation. Still, Levi spoke softly.

"Delbert, you know what Ervin is accused of, right?"

Delbert grinned, "I am. He's a ruthless killer."

"No, Delbert, there's more to it than that. Ervin kills everybody he crosses paths with. He's killed men, women, and children. Ervin doesn't care who he kills; he does it for fun." Levi glanced at the woman and children, lowering his voice to a whisper. "Tommy and I heard they were sending out an experienced group of Marshalls to find him." Levi hesitated. "But no offense to either one of you, but we thought they sent a couple of younger fellas out for the job."

Delbert glanced at Two Dogs. "Even more reason for me and Two Dogs to find him. We still have a few good years left in us."

Tommy nodded. "We would go with you, but once we get this kid to Kingman, we'll be stuck there for a few days. You know how it is. We'll be meeting with the town Sheriff and the good people of the courts. Plus, there's going to be a stack of paperwork waiting. It's not like the old days when we could just drop a man off and leave. Now they want written testimonies detailing everything we did during apprehension and arrest."

Delbert eased back in his seat. "Listen to you, Tommy, you sound like a real educated lawman."

"Got to be; nowadays, the courts want everything detailed down to every last thing said or done; it's a pain in the ass."

Darcy sighed, "So why don't you just cut me loose and save yourselves a lot of headaches."

Levi flicked the side of Darcy's head again, "Shut up, kid; our headache is going to be nothing compared to the pain in the neck you're in store for."

Darcy glanced over his shoulder at Delbert before glaring at the floor.

After many hours of catching up and discussing future plans, the rocking of the train lulled the men to sleep.

The following morning the train squealed into the Kingman train station.

While the passengers gathered their things, the four Lawmen patiently waited for everyone to leave before exiting.

Once outside, Levi and Tommy were greeted by the city Mayor and the Sheriff, along with five deputies. After some handshakes and pats on the back, Levi, Tommy, and Darcy were escorted away. Levi and Tommy waved at Delbert and Two Dogs before they hurried into the station and the teeming streets of Kingman.

Delbert, followed by Two Dogs, stepped directly into the train conductor's office, where Delbert handed the conductor Ervins wanted poster.

"Have you seen this man?"

The chubby conductor squinted over his glasses at Delbert and Two Dogs.

"Nope. Was he traveling with his horse?"

Delbert glanced at Two Dogs. "He was."

The conductor passed Delbert the wanted poster, "Then you might want to check with Dwayne; he's our liveryman. He loads and unloads all checked livestock."

Delbert and Two Dogs tipped their hats before making their way through the bustling crowd to the livery car.

Dwayne was a burly black man dressed in faded blue suspenders and a red flannel that had seen better days.

Delbert and Two dogs waited patiently as Dwayne unloaded the car's horses. Then, after a glance at the proof of ownership paperwork, he returned the horses to their owners.

Once Delbert and Two Dogs' horses were unloaded, Delbert handed Dwayne the wanted poster.

"Have you seen this man?"

Dwayne glanced uninterestedly at the poster before handing it back to Delbert.

"He was here yesterday."

"Did he say where he was headed?"

Dwayne stepped past Delbert and Two Dogs, closing the heavy ramp of the livery car.

"No, sir, I didn't ask."

"Did you happen to see what direction he was heading?"

Dwayne pulled a soiled handkerchief from his front pocket, wiping his brow.

"No sir, it doesn't make no matter to me where anyone was going."

Delbert's patience was running thin. "Did he say anything to you, anything at all?"

Dwayne stepped past Delbert toward the livery barn.

"No sir just handed me his paper and left. There's nothing more to it."

Dwayne waved over his shoulder as he stepped into the barn.

"I got to get back to work."

Delbert glanced at Two Dogs, who was mounting his horse.

"Delbert, we need to get moving."

Delbert folded the wanted poster, placing it in his coat pocket, before mounting his horse.

"Let's check a few saloons. Ervin might have had a dry throat after his travels."

* * *

As they made their way south through the city, Delbert and Two Dogs spoke with several barkeeps and hotel owners; no one claimed to have seen Ervin.

As they continued to the edge of town, Two Dogs squinted southward.

"He's a ghost, Delbert."

"You mentioned that before; what exactly do you mean by a ghost?"

Two Dogs glanced sternly at Delbert.

"He's a ghost. My people believe there are good and evil spirits that walk the earth. This Ervin is an evil spirit, a ghost in a man's body. He travels in both worlds, the spirit and the living, and kills because he hates all things living."

Delbert didn't believe in the supernatural but respected Two Dogs and his beliefs; after all, Delbert's religious beliefs were supported by biblical documentation of Gods and spirits, both good and evil.

"Dogs, I'm not going to deny that Ervin is a ghost, but people have seen him."

"I told you, he is a ghost in a man's body. He is only seen when he chooses to be seen."

Delbert knew there was no need to argue the subject.

"Well, Two Dogs, where do you think an evil spirit would go from here?"

Two Dogs scanned the desert ahead of them.

"The part of the ghost that is still man will travel south. He is going to Mexico, where it's warmer and where he can hide."

Delbert nodded. Two Dogs had an exceptional way of reading a man, even one he had never met. If Two Dogs said Ervin was going to Mexico, then he was going to Mexico.

"Lead the way, Dogs."

Two Dogs quickly examined the hoof-pocked road.

"There are too many tracks. Once we get away from the city, I will find the Ghost's trail."

An hour later, Two Dogs halted his horse.

"Delbert, look, the Ghost left the road. He is crossing the desert."

Delbert searched the road in the direction Two Dogs was pointing. There were a set of hoofprints leaving the soft shoulder of the road.

"That's him, Dogs; there's that drag in the rear hoof."

Two Dogs was well aware of the slight drag mark; his eyes missed nothing.

"He is heading to Mexico. He won't make it before we catch him," said Two Dogs. "The Ghost can't help himself. He will stop to kill on his way. This will slow him."

Delbert knew Two Dogs was right, which sparked a sense of urgency to stop Ervin before any more innocent lives were taken.

The Wicked

Ervin smirked as he rode into the front yard of a small ranch house. Two small boys were too engrossed in playing marbles to notice Ervin until his boot stomped in the center of their circle.

Both boys looked up from their game, alarmed by the sudden intrusion.

Ervin grinned, "Is your ma and pa home?"

The boys stood, dusting themselves off nervously. Neither of them dared to answer the sinister-looking man.

"I asked you a question. What's the matter? Cat, Got your tongues?"

The tallest boy shook his head. "No, sir."

Ervin sighed as he searched the yard.

"What're your names?"

The tallest boy glanced at his little brother.

"My name is David; this is my little brother, Adam."

Ervin grinned, "Well, boys, my name is Ervin; I'm a bible salesman on my way to Mexico. It's been a long ride, so I figured I might as well stop in and see about buying some supper. That is if your ma and pa have any to spare."

David and Adam relaxed. A bible salesman wasn't likely to be a threat.

David pointed at the house.

45

"Ma is out back hanging the laundry. Pa isn't home. He and our uncle Joseph won't be back for a few days. They went to buy some cows."

Ervin beamed, "Well, that sounds real nice, boys. How about you run around back and tell your ma I'm here?"

* * *

Delbert and Two Dogs set up camp near a small spring. Ervin's trail had melted in the darkness, but he had clearly camped in the same spot. He left behind a small fire ring, and suffering from boredom and murderous withdrawals; he scrawled an X into the sand.

"You see that, Delbert? The Ghost is going to kill. He left his mark. Maybe it's a warning."

Delbert untied his bedroll.

"It's not a warning. Ervin is itching to carve his mark into some poor soul's forehead."

Two Dogs pulled out a small bundle of white sage from his saddlebag.

"Delbert, I have to cleanse this place before we sleep. I smell the Ghost's evil."

Delbert picked up his bedroll.

"You probably smell his piss. It's likely he pissed all over the place like a wild animal."

"It's not piss I smell, Delbert. It's the evil he left behind."

Two Dogs lit his sage bundle before chanting and circling their temporary campsite.

Delbert had become accustomed to Two Dog's Sage burning rituals and enjoyed the smell of its smoke. He wasn't sure how something that smelled so pleasant would ward off evil spirits, but apparently, it was a ritual that had been tried and proven for centuries.

When Two Dogs finished chanting, he tossed the rest of the smoldering sage into the fire ring.

"Now we can sleep."

Delbert lit a small fire of twigs before climbing under his blankets. Across from him and silhouetted by the firelight, Delbert noticed Two Dogs staring into the night sky.

"What's the matter, Dogs?"

Two Dogs continued staring at the stars.

"Delbert, the Ghost has killed again."

Delbert sat up. "How do you know? Maybe you're just feeling a bit spooked."

Two Dogs turned his head, facing Delbert.

"Delbert, he has killed again. I hear the cries of the dead."

An uneasy feeling crept like an icy chill into Delbert's spine.

"What do you mean, you hear the cries of the dead?"

"It is something that cannot be explained in words. There is a restlessness in the breeze. Spirits wander when their bodies are taken too soon. That is the only way I can tell you how I know."

Delbert scanned the dancing shadows cast by the firelight.

"We better get him Dogs; he won't stop until he's dead."

Two Dogs agreed, "As soon as there is light to see his trail by, we will leave."

The Return of Coyote

Two Dogs woke to a chattering coyote call. If not for the fact that he had heard the familiar call of coyotes his entire life, he may have thought it was just that. But the chattering call was not the call of a wild coyote; it was a masterfully mimicked call of a human.

Two Dogs sat up; he knew who the call was coming from. He searched the starlit desert landscape for any sign of man but saw nothing. It wasn't until the chattering call resumed that he pinpointed where it was coming from.

Two Dogs stared in the direction of a cluster of small boulders. Two Dogs soon realized the largest boulder was not a boulder but a man. Although darkness concealed his features, Two Dogs recognized him. He was squatting low and motionless, blending in with his surroundings as any Apache warrior would if he didn't want to be seen.

Two Dogs stared at the warrior, as did the warrior at Two Dogs. Several minutes passed with neither warrior moving. Finally, the shadowy warrior stood. He raised his hand over his head so the night sky illuminated his hand sign.

The warrior signed that he was following Two Dogs and Delbert.

Two Dogs signed back, asking why.

The warrior didn't answer; instead, the warrior signed that he would be following Two Dogs staying to the north of him but close enough to keep his eye on him.

Two Dogs signed that he wanted the warrior to leave.

The warrior responded with a mocking howl, which roused several of his hidden pack of coyotes into a frenzy of yelping.

Before running into the darkness with his pack, the warrior again signed that he would follow Two Dogs.

Angered by the warrior, Two Dogs grit his teeth, the warrior had caused him many problems in the past, and now he had returned and would likely cause more, and this time Two Dogs knew that the warrior had become a Spirit Walker.

Two Dogs glanced down at Delbert. He considered waking him but decided doing so would only result in Delbert questioning his sanity.

Aftermath

Two Dogs halted at the top of a grassy hill. Below he spotted two small bodies hanging from a branch in the front yard.

"Delbert, children are hanging in the tree."

Unfortunately, Delbert's vision wasn't as sharp as Two Dogs. He saw a large tree in the front yard of a small house, but nothing hanging in the tree.

"Are you sure, Dogs?"

Two Dogs removed his rifle, followed by Delbert.

"I'm sure, Delbert."

As the two men slowly approached the house, Delbert saw the two small boys hanging by their necks in the tree. As they rode closer, it was evident that both had their tongues cut out and bore the mark of an X on their foreheads.

Delbert and Two Dogs approached the open front door of the house. When they entered, they found the body of a young woman tied to a chair. She, too, had her tongue cut out and had the unmistakable marks of being tortured covering her entire body.

As if to leave a lasting impression on whoever discovered her body, two large knives were left protruding from both sides of her skull, and she, like her boys, was marked with an X on her forehead.

Delbert glanced at the kitchen table, four plates had been made, but only one had been eaten.

"The son of a bitch sat down and ate supper after he killed them," said Delbert.

Two Dogs walked past Delbert. Clearing the two bedrooms of the house before returning.

"It doesn't look like the Ghost took anything."

Delbert poked the food left on one of the plates.

"By the look of things, I'd say Ervin was here a day or so ago."

Two Dogs brushed past Delbert as he stepped towards the front door.

"I'm cutting the boys down and burying them."

Delbert nodded, "I'll untie the woman and bring her out. I think it best we bury them in a single grave. Then I'll head back to town and tell the Sheriff what happened here."

Two Dogs glanced over his shoulder as he walked toward the tree.

"No, Delbert, there isn't time for that. The Ghost is still a day ahead of us. Leave a note."

Delbert thought for a moment. Two Dogs was right; although leaving a note was cold, there was no time to do anything else.

"I feel sorry for the man of the house; I can't imagine what he'll think when he reads the note."

"I don't know, Delbert. Write who we are and tell him we will hunt down the Ghost."

Two hours later, Delbert and Two Dogs rode from the house, leaving behind a note on the kitchen table, and the two boys and their mother were buried beside the tree.

False Profit

Ervin coolly lit a cigar as he looked over the small town of Dripping Springs, New Mexico. The distant lights of the town looked inviting; Ervin briefly considered visiting the town saloon, but he knew that would be foolish. Small towns were dangerous for a wanted man. A man could comfortably blend in with the crowd of a large city or town, but small towns were filled with people who knew each other and where strangers didn't go unseen.

Ervin scanned the outskirts of town before spotting a perfect little place to visit.

As Ervin rode to the gate of the tiny house, he reached into his saddle bag, removing his newly acquired Bible, a parting gift he had awarded himself after killing the small family the day before.

It was a modest little adobe hacienda ringed by cottonwoods, and seated side by side on the front porch as they had every night for many years was an elderly Mexican couple.

Neither of them nor their ancient dog noticed the evil dressed in black at their gate.

"Ah, what a sweet old couple," mused Ervin.

Ervin raised his hand and waved, all the while clutching the Bible.

"Hello there, my children. I am Father Thomas; I have traveled many miles to get here and hoped I could offer you a bible study over supper."

Surprised, both the elderly man and woman stood from their chairs. With their old dog standing stiffly beside them.

The elderly man stepped towards the gate.

"You say you are a priest?"

Ervin innocently smiled, "I am my son; I have traveled many miles from my flock to spread the word of Christ."

The elderly man squinted skeptically.

"I am Hector, and my wife is Lucinda. You were so quiet we didn't see you." Hector glanced over his shoulder at Lucinda. "We don't have very many guests, especially after dark."

Ervin suppressed his annoyance, "I am a man of god, and I'm hungry. Would you turn me away without so much as a piece of bread?"

Hector's eyes widened; he was a devoted man and would never turn away anyone who came to him for food, let alone a man of God.

"Forgive me, Father; please come into our home; we will feed you."

Hector opened the gate for Ervin before shuffling back to the porch.

"Lucinda, heat something for Father Thomas; he has traveled far and is hungry."

Lucinda glanced at Ervin before wrapping her shawl around her shoulders as she shuffled into the house.

Hector waved at Ervin, inviting him to the porch.

"Father, tether your horse to the porch and come inside. You need food and rest."

Ervin knew what he needed, and it had nothing to do with food or rest.

Ervin tipped his hat, "Bless you, Hector; your kindness will be repaid in heaven."

Hector led Ervin into his home. It was a small place with a single bedroom, a kitchen, and a fireplace. Yet even Ervin found it cozy.

Hanging from the open beams in the kitchen were various dried chilies and braids of garlic and onions, and everything had its place.

Lucinda had already started heating tortillas on her wood-burning stove, and judging by the aroma of the little house, Ervin knew Lucinda had mastered the craft of cooking.

Although Ervin wasn't especially hungry, the smell of home cooking aroused his appetite.

Hector smiled as he pulled a chair from the table.

"Please, Father, sit and make yourself comfortable. Our house is your house."

Ervin set the Bible on the table before handing Hector his hat.

"Forgive me; where would you like me to put my hat?"

Hector tenderly took Ervin's hat with both hands and hung it on a peg beside the front door.

"Father, your hat can go where I hang mine."

Ervin smiled, "Sit with me, Hector; let's discuss the scriptures before we eat."

Hector and Lucinda had already had their supper. Still, Hector considered it impolite not to eat with the holy man. Having overheard the conversation and knowing her husband, Lucinda prepared three bowls of beans and a plate of tortillas.

Once Lucinda and Hector were seated, Ervin outstretched his hands, reaching for Lucinda and Hector.

"Let us give thanks for this fine food."

Once they had finished supper, Lucinda cleared the table. When she returned, Ervin reached into his coat pocket, removing a cigar.

Hector glanced at Lucinda.

"You smoke, father?"

Ervin struck a match on the tabletop, lighting the cigar. He gently rolled it between his thumb and index finger, admiring the skillfully wrapped cigar, before taking a long pull of his little treat.

"Yes, Hector, I smoke, not all the time, mind you, but when I can afford a fine cigar, I'll buy one." Ervin grinned. "I'm sorry, Hector, does it bother you that I smoke in your house?"

Hector, flustered, "Oh no, Father, of course not; it's just that I never knew a priest who smoked."

Ervin winked at Hector.

"I do many things," Ervin paused, "I do many things that some would find appalling, but you see Hector, I'm human, and just like everyone else, and I have my shortcomings."

Lucinda eased her chair back from the table. Ervin's tone was unsettling; she began to sense the evil that emanated from Ervin and wanted nothing more than for him to leave. She stood, nervously wringing her hands.

Ervin puffed on his cigar before pointing at Lucinda.

"Lucinda, I prefer you sit still while I'm talking."

Lucinda froze. "Father, I didn't mean to upset you."

Ervin chuckled. "Oh Lucinda, Lucinda, you didn't upset me. You're a sweet old lady, and I am a patient man who is slow to anger. Nothing you could say or do would rile me in the slightest."

Ervin noticed Hector glance past him toward an old shotgun hanging over the front door.

"Hector, you wouldn't be eyeing that shotgun hanging over the door, would you?"

Hector locked eyes with Ervin.

"No, Father."

Ervin smirked, "Hector, I think you're lying. I think you eyed that old bush cannon. I think you would like to grab that old cannon and blow me to kingdom come, and that kind of hurts my feelings."

Ervin gently rolled his cigar. "Hector, I think it's time we got down to business."

Hector shifted nervously.

"Business?"

"Yes, business. See, I'm a firm believer in the old saying that everything happens for a reason, and I honestly think I was sent here to deliver you and Lucinda straight to the pearly gates of heaven. You could call it divine intervention." Ervin paused before puffing on his cigar. "Or you could call it some good old fashion bad luck. Either way, here I am."

Hector reached for Lucinda's hand.

"Father, we are simple people; we don't want any trouble. We took you into our home, fed you, and let you rest, but now I think you should go."

Ervin smirked as he leaned back in his chair.

"Hector, I have no intention of overstaying my welcome. As a matter of fact, I plan on leaving here just as soon as possible. See, I have places to go, things to see. My life is full of promise and future prosperity, while yours." Ervin waved his cigar. "Yours has run its course. So as I said, I have no intention of overstaying my welcome."

Lucinda cleared her throat.

"Then why not leave now, Father? I think you should go."

Ervin grinned as he chewed on his cigar.

"Lucinda, I appreciate your straightforward honesty. I really do, so allow me to extend the same courtesy. I know this may frighten you, but the truth is I'm going to kill you and Hector before I leave."

Lucinda's lips trembled. "Why, Father, why would you want to hurt us? We have done nothing to you."

Smirking, Ervin casually stood from his chair, glaring at Lucinda while casually stroking his chin.

"No, you haven't, you've done nothing at all, but all the same, fate brought us together tonight for a reason."

Ervin stepped behind Hector, resting his hands on his shoulders.

"As I said, I believe I was sent here to deliver your souls to heaven, and one way or another, that's exactly what I intend to do. But, see, I don't shy away from things that have to be done. It's called ethics; when a man feels he has to do something in order to better himself or those around him, he does it, simple as that."

Ervin scanned the house while he gently patted Hector's shoulders. As Ervine glanced around the small house, he noticed a small bucket containing used nails on a small table below the front window.

Resting beside the bucket was a rusty hammer. Ervin grinned.

"Oh, this is perfect, Hector, just perfect; that old bucket of nails just gave me the most wonderful idea."

The old dog woke from his sleep on the porch; although partially deaf, he heard the muffled screams of Lucinda and Hector inside the house.

The porch beneath his frail body shuddered as the calamity inside unfolded. In his younger days, the old dog would have torn the door open to save his family, but in old age, bravado had been replaced by an overabundance of caution. So instead, he stood on stiff wobbly legs and limped into the darkness.

The Spirit Walker and Coyote

Delbert and Two Dogs followed Ervin's trail to a small ranch house outside Dripping Springs. As they approached, it was evident that something disastrous had transpired.

The town's sickly, hollow-cheeked undertaker and another man were unloading two coffins from the back of a wagon while the town's elderly Sheriff and a portly red-cheeked priest stood at the open door of the house.

A dozen locals were lined up at the gate, soberly gawking at the spectacle as it unfolded. It appeared to Two Dogs and Delbert as if all of them were in a state of shock and confusion, as none were speaking.

No one other than the Sheriff noticed Delbert and Two Dogs as they approached.

Two Dogs glanced at Delbert, "The Ghost has killed again."

"Yes, he has," Delbert sighed, "Dogs, this man is pure evil. He's killed far more people than the few he's been accused of. He has no control of himself."

Two Dogs disagreed. "The Ghost has control of himself; that's why he is still killing. He is clever; If he did not have control of himself, he would already be dead. Delbert, only a fool would underestimate what the Ghost is capable of doing."

Two Dogs glanced down; Ervin's trail had become obscured by the many hoofs and footprints left by the townspeople.

"Delbert, I do not need to go to the house."

Two Dogs leaned low in his saddle, examining the partially obscured tracks of Ervin's horse.

"I will circle around back and find the Ghost's trail."

Delbert agreed; there was no need for both of them to confirm what they had already suspected. Finding Ervin's tracks was more important than seeing the carnage he had left behind. All the same, Delbert was keeping a running tally of Ervin's victims, not that it mattered. Ervin had already received the death penalty by hanging, and as Delbert knew, you can only hang a man once, regardless of how many crimes he committed.

As Delbert brushed past the gawking townspeople gathered at the gate, the Sheriff eyed him suspiciously. Undeterred, Delbert opened the gate and introduced himself.

"Sheriff, my name is Marshall Crenshaw. What happened here?"

The Sheriff extended his hand, firmly shaking Delbert's hand.

"Nice to meet you, Marshall; I'm Sheriff Little. To answer your question, what happened here is a double murder of two of the nicest people I ever knew."

Sheriff Little scratched his head; he was confused as to why a Marshall could have already been dispatched to Dripping Springs.

Delbert tipped his hat, "I'm sorry to hear that, Sheriff. My partner and I are tracking the man who may have done this. Did either of the victims have an X carved on their foreheads?"

Sheriff Little nodded toward the door, "Go in and see for yourself."

Delbert respectfully removed his hat before entering the house.

Inside were the bodies of Hector and Lucinda. Both were seated at the kitchen table, with their hands nailed palms up on the tabletop, their heads facing up to the ceiling, their throats cut from ear to ear, and Ervin's signature X carved into their foreheads.

Delbert glanced at the Sheriff, and the priest, standing side by side in the doorway.

"Sheriff, this is the work of Ervin Wells. He is a cold-blooded murderer with an insatiable appetite for killing. He was sentenced to death by hanging for six other murders, but he escaped a Sheriff's transport wagon a while back and killed both deputies while he was at it."

Sheriff Little sighed, "Well, this Ervin Wells killed two good people. I looked around; it didn't look like he had taken anything; he just killed them."

Sheriff Little choked. " They didn't deserve to die like this."

"That's what he does, Sheriff. Robbery isn't what he's interested in; it's killing. He kills because he's evil; he enjoys it."

Sheriff Little sighed, "Well, Marshall, I hope you catch up to him and kill him. I wish I could help, but this is a small town with hard-working, simple people. No one is willing to form a posse and go after him. The only one man enough to volunteer was Hector and Lucinda's thirteen-year-old grandson Carlos. He's the one who found them this morning."

Delbert stepped past Sheriff Little and the priest as he exited the house.

"You tell Carlos I appreciate his courage, but it would be best if he stays in town."

Sheriff Little nodded, "He already left, the kids got an eye for tracking, and there was no stopping him."

Delbert's face flushed, "Sheriff, how long ago did he leave?"

Sheriff Little opened his pocket watch, "About five hours ago."

"Sweet Jesus, Sheriff, if he isn't already dead, he will be soon. I'll send him home if he's still alive."

Delbert stepped briskly to his horse before sending it galloping to the back of the house.

When Delbert reached the backside of the house, he discovered that Two Dogs had found Ervin's trail and was a mere speck trailed by a ribbon of dust in the distance.

Delbert spurred his horse forward, reaching Two Dogs within a minute.

"Dogs, we have a serious problem. Ervin killed an old man and woman back there, and according to the Sheriff, their thirteen-year-old grandson is tracking Ervin alone."

Two Dogs calmly shielded his eyes with his hand as he looked southward.

"I knew someone was tracking the Ghost; there were many crisscrossing trails before he found the Ghost's tracks." Two Dogs pointed at the hoofprints. "As you can see, he pursued the Ghost riding fast."

Delbert examined the hoofprints; he shuddered at the thought of what Ervin may do to the boy. Although Delbert was a hardened Lawman, he had a soft spot for children he always had, and knowing a thirteen-year-old boy was alone tracking a ruthless killer terrified him.

"We need to hurry, Dogs; Ervin will kill that boy."

"We will hurry, but not so much as to wear our horses. If the boy caught up with the Ghost, he is already dead."

Two Dogs nudged his horse forward at an even trot, he knew the odds of the boy still being alive were slim, and although the boy had honorable intentions, they were poorly planned.

* * *

Dusk came quickly, and with it came darkness which melted Ervin and Carlos' tracks into obscurity.

Rather than taking the chance of losing the trail and wandering into the desert, Two Dogs halted.

"Delbert, we have to stop; I can't track in this darkness."

As much as Delbert wished they could continue, he knew Two Dogs was right.

"I hope that boy hasn't caught up with Ervin."

Unless Carlos had somehow veered off Ervin's trail, Two Dogs was confident Carlos had succeeded in catching up with Ervin and was most likely dead.

"So do I; his death will not be quick. Out here, there will be no one to stop him. The Ghost will take his time with the boy."

Delbert doubted Ervin was concerned about anyone being out here. He would take his time killing the boy if for no other reason than he liked to.

"Ervin doesn't care if people are around or not; he took his time with the old man and woman in Dripping Springs."

Delbert reflected on what he saw in the house. During the many years he had served as a Marshall, he had seen death and atrocity the likes no human should ever be exposed to, but age was catching up to him. Things that didn't used to bother him bothered him now.

"Dogs, he cut their throats and nailed their hands to the kitchen table. I wish I hadn't gone in there."

Two Dogs shrugged. "You had to know if it was the work of the Ghost. You had no choice."

Delbert shrugged, but it doesn't make what I saw any easier.

Two Dogs removed his bedroll from his saddle. He had seen and taken part in many killings as a warrior, but he did so while waging an unofficial war to save his people and their native land. Still, he understood how the horrors of murder and human carnage were impossible to erase from memory, and he, like Delbert, often found those memories coming back to haunt him as he aged.

Although Delbert felt childish, he spread his bedroll beside Two Dogs. A move that didn't go unnoticed by Two Dogs.

Two Dogs grinned at his old friend. He knew that even the bravest of men sometimes needed reassurance and a place where they felt safe to rest.

"Delbert, when I was leading my warriors, there was a man we called Coyote. He was a brave and reckless warrior. He troubled me with his ways. Coyote was like the Ghost; he liked to kill, even if the people were not enemies of the Apache. I warned him many times to stop, but Coyote would not listen. One day, my warriors spotted seven white men using their pans in the waters. These seven men did not know the danger they were in. I knew this because my warriors said these men did not guard their camp. I told my warriors to leave them be; starting a war with the whites would end us. My warriors listened, except for one, Coyote left our camp in the night. He found these white men and killed them. When he bragged about what he had done, I made him leave, but he followed us, causing many troubles. In the night, he made the calls of the wild Coyote, but we knew it was him, and we knew he had made peace with a pack of coyotes and was now the leader of his dog warriors. Soon we learned how badly he angered the whites when he killed the seven. Greene's Soldiers hunted us for many days until we could go no further. That is when the battle was fought. We killed some, and they killed some, but in the end, they forced us to surrender. Only a few escaped, the rest were hanged, and they took me prisoner. I never saw the Coyote again, but I knew when he was near. He is a spirit walker, half man, half spirit, just like this Ghost."

Delbert nervously scanned the darkness. With everything he had seen, the last thing he wanted to hear was Two Dogs' stories about the undead.

"Dogs, was that story supposed to make me feel better about this situation? Because if it was, you didn't make me any more comfortable than I was five minutes ago. As a matter of fact, you just made everything worse."

Two Dogs chuckled. "Delbert, what I told you is not a story; it is fact. Spirit Walkers are real, and the Ghost is one of them. We will catch him and kill the body that carries the spirit, but we will never stop the spirit. Instead, it will find another body and become a Spirit Walker again."

Delbert rolled onto his side, staring into the darkness.

"That's great, Dogs; thank you for sharing that. Now I'll have no problem sleeping."

Two Dogs sat up, "Delbert, I will burn sage; it will protect you while you sleep."

Delbert grunted, "I'd appreciate that, Dogs, and while you're at it, how about handing me a fistful of that stuff so I can fill my pockets?"

Two Dogs grinned as he climbed out from under his blanket. Although he hadn't intended to frighten Delbert, Two Dogs knew he had. It amused him; he considered Delbert his brother and the bravest man he had ever met. But he inadvertently learned Delbert's one shortcoming. Delbert feared the spirit world. It was a fear that perplexed Two Dogs; most White men refused to say they believed in spirits, yet when faced with them, they were terrified. He wondered how a man could fear something he denied existed. It was a mystery that Two Dogs had no doubt he would ever solve.

After cleansing the campsite with the smoldering sage, Two Dogs lie down and stared into the starry sky. He remembered as a child; his father would point to the different constellations, reciting ancient stories of creation and mythical tales of the sky gods. It pained him to see his father's face and still clearly recall the sound of his voice.

His father had taught him everything related to being a boy, but there were many lessons he never had the chance to teach him. His father was shot in the back and killed by a Mexican cattle rancher who had trespassed onto Apache territory.

Although the rancher died at the hands of his father's warriors, it wasn't how it was supposed to end. Two Dogs' father rode onto the rancher's property in broad daylight, intending to warn the rancher to keep his cattle off Apache land. The rancher refused, retreating into his home and retrieving a rifle.

As Two Dogs father and his warriors were leaving, the rancher shot Two Dogs father in the back, and thus the undeclared war began.

Two Dogs closed his eyes. The memories of raids, blood, and death haunted him. He and his warriors had committed murder similar to how Ervin did. The exception was they did it to instill fear. All the land grabbers had to do was respect the boundaries of Apache land, and then the killing would stop, but they didn't; they simply kept coming, wave after wave of them, and no amount of killing seemed to deter them.

Two Dogs cleared his mind; he had to before the memories of the past overwhelmed him. When sleep finally came, it was restless, the kind of sleep that provided no relief from exhaustion.

* * *

Delbert woke; the moon had risen late, dimly lighting the surrounding desert in a silvery light. Beside him, Two Dogs mumbled something in his sleep.

As Delbert sat up, he listened as the cool desert breeze whispered through the surrounding creosote. It was a harsh, unforgiving landscape, but it was tolerable in the dead of night, and to Delbert, it was beautiful.

Delbert glanced at Two Dogs; he considered waking him, but it was still too dark to continue their pursuit. Plus, he figured a few more hours of sleep was exactly what he needed.

As Delbert lay down, a shadow in the distance caught his attention. A man silhouetted by the moon appeared to be squatting atop a boulder, his features obscured by the dark.

Delbert squinted, unsure if his eyes were playing tricks on him or if he was dreaming.

The figure turned his head upwards before howling the call of the Coyote. The combination of howling, whining, and laughter sounded no different than that of an alpha male calling his pack, and his pack responded.

In the distance, the cackling whine of coyotes echoed through the desert as they responded dutifully to the alpha. Their crazed cackles grew louder as they approached, taking on a frenzied chorus as they crossed the desert.

Then as suddenly as they started, the chorus abruptly silenced. Delbert slowly reached for his rifle as he stared at the distant shadow; if it was a fight the shadow wanted, then Delbert was more than ready to deliver.

The shadow remained motionless. Although Delbert couldn't see his eyes, he knew the shadow was watching him.

Soon the ghostly figures of two coyotes jumped onto the boulder, sitting on either side of the shadow. Delbert had seen enough; he reached for Two Dogs, startling him from a troubled sleep.

Two Dogs leaped from his blankets, rifle in hand.

"What is it, Delbert?"

Delbert glanced at Two Dogs before pointing in the shadow's direction, but the shadow was gone. Only the faintly lit boulder remained.

"Dogs, I saw a man sitting on that boulder. Didn't you hear him? He was howling like a coyote, and he wasn't alone."

Two Dogs searched in the direction Delbert had pointed.

"How many men were there?"

"None; he had a pack of coyotes with him." Delbert instantly knew how ridiculous he sounded, but Two Dogs didn't appear surprised.

Two Dogs lowered his rifle. He knew Delbert had seen Coyote and understood his fear.

"You saw the Spirit Walker Coyote. It is following us and the Ghost."

Delbert regretted waking Two Dogs; the last thing he wanted to do was discuss Spirit Walkers. And now that he was wide awake, he was sure the entire thing had been a nightmare spawned from Two Dogs' ghost stories.

Delbert lay down, covering himself to his nose under his blankets.

"Dogs, it was a bad dream, I don't want to talk about anymore Spirit Walkers, ghosts, or anything remotely related to the subject."

Two Dogs brushed Delbert's comment off; he was confused.

"I have never heard of a white man seeing a Spirit Walker, but now that you have, you cannot deny they are real."

Delbert rolled onto his side, "I'm serious, Dogs; I don't want to talk about that anymore."

Undeterred, Two Dogs continued, "I think the Spirit Walker will cause us problems."

Or maybe I had a nightmare."

"No, Delbert, it was not a nightmare; it wanted you to see him. It is Coyote; he revealed himself to me. He said he is following us but would not say why."

Delbert raised his hand, "Dogs, enough. I told you I don't want to hear anything else about it."

Two Dogs stared into the darkness, searching for any sign of the Spirit Walker, but the spirit had moved on.

"Delbert, I will burn Sage, then you will feel better."

Delbert pretended he was sleeping; he knew his old friend well. If he said another word, Two Dogs would begin a lengthy discussion on the subject, a subject Delbert felt better suited for daylight hours.

Deadly Mistake

Carlos jumped from his old horse, rifle in hand. He was ready to kill.

The tracks of the killer led to a cluster of boulders where he was sure the killer was hiding.

Anger had replaced fear and, with it, irrationality. He had no idea who he was up against or how efficient the killer might be. All Carlos knew was whoever he was up against had killed the two people who had practically raised him.

The morning he had found his slaughtered grandparents, Carlos had gotten up early, as he did every morning, to help his grandfather with his morning chores. The day had started as it always had. He fed his grandfather's chickens, gathered wood for his grandmother's stove, and opened the barn. The only thing that was out of the ordinary was the old family dog was nowhere to be seen.

Worried, Carlos searched the barn for the old dog before finally finding him cowering behind a bale of alfalfa. Then, fearing the old dog may be injured, he went to the house to get his grandfather.

As Carlos approached the house, he noticed the front door was ajar, but the house was silent. He carefully set down an armful of stovewood before cautiously pushing the door open.

That's when he found them; Carlos froze in the doorway, unable to comprehend what he was seeing.

Fear, followed by anger, overcame him; Carlos fled the house, running to the Sheriff's Office for help.

When he burst through the door of the Sheriff's Office, he startled Sheriff Little, who was just preparing his morning coffee. Sheriff Little knew something terrible had happened by the look on Carlos' face. He had seen the same expression years earlier when an elderly woman named Lupe had burst through his door after finding her husband crushed under his wagon.

Carlos could not speak; he stood in the doorway in shock, only e pointing toward his grandparent's house.

As the Sheriff and Carlos rushed back to the little house, several townspeople noticed the commotion and followed.

The sight that awaited them shocked even the hardiest of souls when they arrived. Nothing like what happened inside the little house had ever happened before, and for those who saw it, it was forever etched into their minds.

After the gruesome discovery, Sheriff Little desperately tried to muster a few men to assist him in tracking the killer, but no one was willing to help. They, like the Sheriff, were too frightened to hunt the person responsible for the killings. All except for Carlos, who wasted no time grabbing his grandfather's old rifle and riding his old horse in the direction the killer's tracks led.

Carlos crawled on his stomach to a cluster of small boulders. He caught up with the man who killed his grandparents, and soon the man would pay for his evil deed.

Carlos brought his grandfather's old, battered rifle to a shooting position before peering down its rusty barrel toward the killers' campsite, but the killer was nowhere to be seen. Only his horse was visible, grazing lazily on the sun-scorched desert weeds.

Carlos scanned the surrounding boulders, but the killer had either hidden or found a place in the rocks to relieve himself. Either way, Carlos knew he had the upper hand, and the moment he had a clear shot, he intended to kill the man who killed his grandparents.

Several minutes passed, and still, the killer did not appear. Carlos considered positioning himself closer, lessening the chance of missing his target, when a boot from behind pinned him to the ground, followed by a rifle barrel to the back of his head.

"Well, hello there, little boy; you looking for someone?"

* * *

Delbert and Two Dogs spotted a riderless horse in the distance.

"Ervin got him," Delbert sighed; he had hoped to reach the kid and send him home before he got himself killed.

"Damn it, Dogs, there's no way that isn't the kid's horse."

Two Dogs nodded, "It is an old workhorse." Two Dogs shielded his eyes as he scanned the surrounding desert. "The boy is nowhere."

Carlos' horse walked head down past Delbert and Two Dogs as it made its weary trip back home, still carrying a cracked and weathered saddle that had seen better days some twenty years prior.

Delbert and Two Dogs continued, hoping the old horse would make it home.

"Delbert, my people believe all living things have spirits. The old horse walked with a heavy heart. It feels the loss of his owner."

"I believe the same thing, and I agree. I think the horse saw what happened and is grieving. I wasn't much of a believer in that until Jose's horse wouldn't leave the spot where you cremated him. Do you remember that Dogs?"

"I remember." Jose was a subject that Two Dogs preferred to keep from discussing. He felt responsible for what happened to Jose and knew he would live with that guilt for the rest of his life.

Two Dogs changed the subject.

"Delbert, we should ride through the night. The moon will be late, but it will be more than half full. So we will rest when it is dark and wait for it to rise."

Delbert glanced at the sun, "That's going to be a long time off. But, hopefully, we can close the gap on that son of bitch."

Two Dogs spotted something in the distance; he leaned forward in his saddle, concentrating on the mysterious movements ahead. Then it came to him; he knew what he was seeing.

Delbert glanced at Two Dogs, "What do you see, Dogs?"

"Far ahead, I see birds, blackbirds; they are on the ground."

"Blackbirds?"

Two Dogs nodded, "Vultures."

* * *

Ervin rode south, smirking as he relived his deeds from the day before. What had started as just another day on a dusty ride ended with what he considered a stroke of good luck. Perhaps a gift. Whatever it was was utterly unexpected and cherished.

As Ervin unknowingly approached the small town of Borrego, he had the unsettling feeling that he was being watched. By who or what, he wasn't sure, but whatever it was made the hair on the back of his neck rise.

With the same nagging feeling of being watched, Ervin continued another mile before seeing a coyote run across the rutted road in front of him.

Whether day or night, seeing a lone coyote in the desert wasn't anything concerning to Ervin, but seconds later, a second and then a third coyote darted across the road before disappearing into the scattered Ocotillo cactus.

Ervin stopped his horse when a fourth coyote darted from the shoulder of the road and stopped. It was a massive male that showed no sign of giving ground to Ervin.

Ervin grinned as he reached for his rifle; if the coyote wanted to challenge him, Ervin would end the standoff on his terms.

Before Ervin had time to unsheath the rifle, an Apache warrior stepped from behind a boulder and stood beside the Coyote. The warrior's clothes were the color of the coyote, and his presence did not appear to disturb the coyote.

Ervin slowly removed his rifle from its sheath, never taking his eyes off the warrior and the coyote. Before he could raise his rifle into firing position, the warrior crouched, grabbing a handful of sand.

As the warrior stood, he raised his fist towards Ervin. Sand trickled between the warrior's hand, obscuring his feet in a cloud of dust. The warrior grinned before opening his hand. He blew the sand toward Ervin.

Ervin's horse reeled as the small handful of sand culminated into a swirling cloud. Then, without warning, Ervin's horse bolted blindly off the road, with Ervin struggling to remain saddled.

Hearing the coyotes howling behind him, Ervin glanced over his shoulder. All four wild dogs were behind his horse, gnashing at her rear hooves with rabid determination.

Although unnecessary, Ervin spurred the old horse to run faster. Within minutes the coyotes turned and trotted back in the direction from which they had come.

Ervin slowed his exhausted horse, patting her neck to assure her the danger had passed. He tried rationalizing what had happened but could think of nothing that could reasonably explain what had occurred.

As Ervin continued south, he repeatedly glanced over his shoulders, expecting to see the coyotes and the warrior; to his relief, they were nowhere to be seen. In the end, Ervin ruled out seeing the warrior. The warrior was a figment of his imagination. As for the coyotes, they were either rabid or starving and had mistaken Ervin's horse for an easy meal.

With the incident worked out and resolved, Ervin relaxed. Searching the desert ahead, he spotted a grove of cottonwoods at the base of a deep canyon. Above the cottonwoods, the landscape was green, dotted with oak and pine.

Ervin made his decision; he would cut through the forest and enjoy the coolness of its shade. A reprieve from the desert landscape would be a welcome change from the desert heat.

As Ervin rode slowly towards the cottonwood grove, he realized how deceptive the desert could be when judging distance. As he approached the welcoming shade of the woods, it seemed it was matching his progress and retreating from him.

A half-hour passed since Ervin rode toward the Cottonwood grove. When finally he found himself under the shade of the cottonwoods, Ervin watered his thirsty horse in a clear stream while taking a few moments to fill his canteens and wash the desert sand from his face.

As he inspected the area, he noticed signs of a native camp. Several fire rings, including a few shattered ollas, were scattered throughout the woods.

The site was not a permanent village site; instead, it appeared to Ervin as if it were a hunting camp or waypoint to rest.

Within minutes Ervin's suspicions were proven correct. He spotted a well-groomed path led from the grove's west end, extending up the canyon in a westerly direction. This was the site for natives to camp before traversing up the canyon and a place to water their horses and rest before leaving the canyon and traveling back to their desert villages.

Ervin glanced up into the canopy of shimmering leaves. The sun was high, allowing for hours of travel. He decided to continue up the canyon and avoid running into a traveling clan of natives.

The trail proved easy to traverse, and after several hours he found himself surrounded by a beautiful forest that even he, an evil monster, could appreciate.

Ervin made camp that evening in a small clearing. After building a small fire, he lay on his blanket, staring at a cloudless starry sky and comforted by the memory of his latest killing.

Although wanted by the Law, Ervin had no plans of turning over a new leaf; he figured if he played his cards right, Mexico would be his next hunting ground. It would be a land of opportunity and a place where no one knew who he was or what he had done.

Ervin lit a cigar and thought, "Life was going to be good."

Delbert and Two Dogs soon discovered why the vultures had gathered where they had.

Carlos lay face up, stripped to the waist. Ervin had staked him to the ground spread eagle by his wrists and ankles before Ervin had flayed Carlos from the base of his ribcage to his waist, disemboweling him like a fish.

Vultures swarmed Carlos' body, grotesquely tugging at his intestine as they greedily fought among one another over their hellish feast.

As Delbert and Two Dogs approached Carlos' corpse, the vultures croaked, spreading their wings, but refused to flee from their grisly feast.

Delbert glanced at Carlos' rifle, which was rammed into the ground barrel first beside Carlos' X-carved head as if it were a grave marker.

Delbert glanced from Carlos' mutilated body toward Two Dogs.

"I guess Ervin didn't need the rifle."

"The Ghost has everything he needs." Two Dogs pointed to Ervin's tracks. "He is going west; we have to keep moving."

As he followed Two Dogs, Delbert glanced at the grotesque spectacle.

"I hate leaving the kid like this."

Two Dogs glanced over his shoulder. "Delbert, there is no time; the Ghost is heading towards Borego.

Delbert knew Two Dogs was right; they had to continue. They had old friends in the small desert town of Borrego, namely Mason Hill. The man Two Dogs and Delbert had hunted until discovering Mason was pardoned.

With a final glance, Delbert followed Two Dogs west, leaving the vultures to their feast.

The Warriors Morning Bird and Meniish

Late that night, Delbert and Two Dogs halted their horses. In the distance, the scattered lights of Borego twinkled peacefully.

Delbert shifted in his saddle. "Dogs, I can't see a damn thing. Does it look like Ervin went into town?"

"No, the Ghost is traveling south." Two Dogs pointed to the ground. "He veered away; maybe he has decided not to be seen."

Two Dogs rode forward, noticing the coyote tracks and what appeared to be the trail of a powerful dust devil.

Delbert noticed Two Dogs' intense focus on the road.

"What's the matter, Dogs?"

Two Dogs pointed to the ground. "Something happened here. There are the tracks of coyotes."

Delbert shrugged. "Dogs, there are coyote tracks all over this desert."

"No, Delbert, there is more than just coyote tracks. There was a powerful wind that started and ended here. The wind blew in your direction and nowhere else."

Delbert knew a lesson of the supernatural was coming next.

"Dogs, we've got to get moving. Ervin's tracks are right here, heading south. So let's get moving."

Just as Delbert expected, Two Dogs circled his horse around the blown sand.

"Delbert, it was the Spirit Walker Coyote. He crossed paths with Ervin, and then he forced him away from Borego."

Delbert shrugged. "Maybe he has gotten his fill of killing for a while and figured he'd skip Borrego.."

Two Dogs veered off the sandy road, following Ervin's trail.

"The Ghost will never get his fill of killing."

That was the end of the discussion.

Delbert followed Two Dogs southward, pausing as he glanced over his shoulder. He wondered what the ranch hands at Jack's ranch would think if they knew he and Two Dogs were in the area again.

His and Two Dogs' last appearance didn't go so well. Three of the ranch hands had been killed, and even though Delbert knew it had nothing to do with his and Two Dogs' arrival, the lead ranch hand, Jason Mathiot, didn't feel that way.

In the end, Delbert and Two Dogs left Mason's adoptive Kumeyaa clan with a declaration of pardon and returned home. Unfortunately, this was after a bounty hunter had shot Mason in the back.

Delbert continued following Two Dogs, listening as Two Dogs softly sang an Apache warrior song.

Delbert often wondered what Two Dogs was singing about but never asked. He figured if Two Dogs wanted him to know, he would tell him.

* * *

As the sun arose and began casting its silvery glow in the east, Two Dogs veered westward, following Ervin's trail.

"Delbert, the Ghost is heading toward the canyon."

Delbert eyed the familiar landscape ahead. He and Two Dogs were escorted up the canyon six months earlier by a Kumeyaay elder and healer named Broken Leg. Broken Leg led them to the Kumeyaay summer village site, where Mason had been living a peaceful life with his pregnant Kumeyaay wife.

The trail leading up the canyon was a well-known trade route and shortcut used by the Kumeyaay and the Cahuilla peoples. It also doubled as an easy-access route to the Kumeyaay summer village site. A sight that had been seasonally occupied for countless generations.

Two Dogs squinted as he focused at the base of the trailhead.

Two Dogs spotted a thin thread of smoke drifting among the canopy of the trees.

"Delbert, there is someone ahead."

Delbert strained to see anything or anyone in the pale morning light.

"Dogs, I don't see anything."

Concentrating on the grove, Two Dogs realized there was more than one person.

"There are many people; I see them."

Delbert removed his rifle from its sheath, laying it on his lap.

Two Dogs glanced at Delbert.

"Delbert put the rifle away. If these people wanted to harm us, they already would have."

Delbert shrugged, "How do you figure Dogs? They're too far ahead to shoot at us."

Two Dogs raised his right hand, signaling Delbert to keep his eyes ahead.

"There are two scouts close by, one on the left, one on the right."

Delbert fought the urge to turn and look.

"Are they armed?"

Two Dogs nodded. "They are carrying bows. I recognize them; they are Kumeyaay. They are Mason's people. We will be okay; they know who we are."

The Clan began walking up the canyon as Delbert as Two Dogs approached the cottonwood grove. Two warriors remained in the grove, waiting for Delbert and Two Dogs' arrival.

Morning Bird rode from the grove before flanking to the right of Delbert and Two Dogs while his second in command, Meniish, flanked to the left. Although the warriors recognized the two Lawmen, neither trusted them. They had learned that the appearance of White men often resulted in trouble.

Although the warriors' horses were trained to move silently, neither of the warriors hid themselves. As the warriors rode toward Delbert and Two Dogs, they stared blankly. Both warriors had been taught not to show emotion to strangers, especially if they weren't sure what the strangers' intentions were.

Fifty yards from the grove, Two Dogs stopped his horse and stood, arms extended to his sides, with his hands palms up.

Morning Bird rode toward Delbert and Two Dogs while Meniish remained stationary.

Morning Bird stopped his horse twenty feet from Two Dogs. He glared at Two Dogs but said nothing.

Two Dogs lowered his arms, confident he had made his peaceful intentions clear.

"I remember you, Morning Bird. Me and the Marshall are tracking a killer. His tracks lead to the canyon where your people are traveling."

Morning Bird glanced over his right shoulder toward the canyon trail.

"Why is this man traveling to our summer camp?"

"I do not know if he is traveling to your summer camp. I won't know this unless you let us pass."

Morning Bird nudged his horse forward, pacing it from left to right.

"I will let you follow this man you seek, but I will ride with you. Meniish will lead us up the trail, and Nemas and Muu will follow."

Delbert glanced to his right; Muu appeared, riding his horse from behind a boulder. From Delbert's left, Nemas appeared. Both warriors' expressions were stoic and blank.

Delbert wasn't sure if he should wave or sit still. Finally, it was Morning Bird who broke the tension.

"Marshall, come, we are traveling with you to the top of the canyon."

Delbert cautiously rode his horse alongside Two Dogs while Morning Bird aligned himself with Delbert.

Morning Bird pointed toward the trail.

"Two Dogs go."

Two Dogs nodded before leading the group to the trail.

As the group slowly ascended the canyon, several awkward minutes passed before Morning Bird broke the silence.

"Mason's child was born."

Delbert nodded. " I'm happy to hear that. Is it a boy or girl?"

Morning Bird smiled; he was happy for Mason and Gabriella.

"It was a boy, Mason and Gabriella have given him two names, but Gabriella has not told us which name to use."

"Two names?"

"Two names, Mason and Nyemii. In our language, Nyemii means bobcat."

"I like that. Both names are good."

Delbert hesitated, "So Mason survived the shooting?"

Morning Bird nodded. "He lived but was not well to travel when my people returned to the winter camp; Mason and Gabriella stayed in the mountains."

Two Dogs glanced at Delbert. Delbert knew they were both thinking the same thing. If Ervin had somehow crossed paths with Mason, Ervin was either dead or had killed Mason.

Several hours later, they reached the top of the trail, where they found the Kumeyaay Clan resting peacefully under the trees in a lush pine and oak tree wooded meadow.

Manuel, the Clans Chief, spotted the warriors along with Delbert and Two Dogs. Morning Bird halted the group while he rode ahead to speak with Manuel.

Manuel eyed Morning suspiciously.

"Morning Bird, what is this? Why are they here?"

Morning Bird glanced over his shoulder toward Delbert and Two Dogs.

"They are not here for Mason. They are tracking another man. This man they seek traveled the same path we have taken. They asked if they could pass."

Manuel sighed; up until six months earlier, there had never been so many issues arise during the migration. He longed for the days when he and his people could travel into their ancestral mountain camp without the interference of white men and the troubles they seemed to bring.

"Tell them to come to me."

Morning Bird waved at his group of warriors, beckoning them to approach.

Meniish nodded, he had no idea how this encounter with Manuel would unfold, but he and the other warriors were ready for whatever the outcome may bring.

"Manuel wants to speak to you," said Meniish. Meniish's tone was friendly but firm, warning Delbert and Two Dogs not to step out of line.

Delbert and Two Dogs obeyed and respectfully dismounted and walked to where Manuel stood. As they did so, the rest of the clan prepared to continue their journey. Except for Jack, an overweight white man who had married into the Clan, Jack had met the two Lawmen when they arrived at the summer camp six months earlier. Although he was happy to see them, he wondered why they had reappeared on Kumeyaay land again.

Manuel grinned at Delbert and Two Dogs.

"It is good to see you. But, unfortunately, Morning Bird tells me you are hunting a killer."

Two Dogs nodded. "Yes, we have been tracking this man for many days. He took the canyon trail; that is why we are here."

Manuel glanced at Morning Bird. "This man you are hunting, where is he going?"

"We do not know, but we must find his trail soon. This man will kill anyone he sees, including the Kuymeyaay people. He is a Spirit Walker."

Manuel squinted, the Kumeyaay had stories of evil spirits, but this confused him.

"Is this a man you are hunting or a spirit?"

Two Dogs decided to forgo a lesson in the supernatural and describe a Spirit Walker in basic terms.

"This man is both, his body is that of a man, but his soul is that of an evil spirit. He walks in both worlds; he is a ghost."

Manuel glanced at Morning Bird before speaking to him in Yuman.

"What is this Apache talking about? Do you think he and Delbert have lost their minds?"

Morning Bird and his warriors laughed, which unsettled Delbert. Although they had left the Kumeyaay people on good terms months earlier, they were initially greeted with hostility. Nevertheless, he hoped this meeting would end on a friendly note, without bloodshed.

"Manuel, they are crazy; there is no man spirit. Let them track this Spirit Walker."

"Maybe they will track this Spirit to the ocean; then they will have to swim to catch him." Manuel laughed. "I will let them cross our mountain."

Manuel reverted to speaking English.

"Two Dogs, you and Delbert can cross our mountain. I hope you find your Spirit Walker."

Two Dogs relaxed; he feared the outcome wouldn't have been desirable.

Two Dogs nodded before he and Delbert mounted their horses and carefully passed the gawking Clan.

Jack cheerfully waved at them before his Kumeyaay wife, Kyla, slapped his hand.

"Jack stop that; you act like you are a child. You do not know what was discussed."

Jack's face burned red, embarrassed by Kyla's reprimand. It was a well-known fact that Kyla loved Jack more than anything else, but she constantly scolded him in front of the rest of the Clan.

Manuel glanced toward Kyla and Jack before shaking his head. It seemed Jack could never get through the day without doing something to anger his wife.

Manuel cleared his throat. "Morning Bird, you and Meniish follow them until they are many miles from here."

Morning Bird and Meniish nodded, Manuel had spoken, and his orders would be obeyed.

Morning Bird spoke to Manuel in Yuman. "Manuel, only one question."

"What is it, Morning Bird?"

"If there are problems, what would you have us do?"

Manuel understood his warrior's eagerness to fight but waved Morning Bird off.

"There will be no problems. But, if there is, I forbid you to kill them. Defend yourselves if you must, but do not harm them. They may be crazy, but they are Lawmen. Killing them would bring great troubles to us."

Morning Bird and Meniish were disappointed, but they knew Manuel was right.

* * *

A mile west of the Clan, Two Dogs found Ervin's tracks. The tracks took a southerly turn toward the Clan's summer campsite.

"Delbert, the Ghost, is traveling towards the Kumeyaay summer camp. If he sees Mason and his family, he will kill them."

Delbert glanced back at the Morning Bird and Meniish, who were following a distance behind.

"I will tell the warriors."

Two Dogs turned in his saddle, waving his arms at Morning Bird and Meniish.

Morning Bird and Meniish stopped, unsure why Two Dogs motioned for them to approach him.

"Morning Bird, what are the crazy men doing?"

Morning Bird shrugged. "I don't know, you can never judge what a crazy man will do, and now there are two."

Meniish nervously felt for his knife handle for reassurance.

Morning Bird glanced at Meniish. "Do not pull your knife, not yet. Go to the right of Delbert; I will go left to Two Dogs."

Delbert and Two Dogs watched as Morning Bird and Meniish cautiously rode toward them. Two Dogs recognized the look of apprehension on both warriors' faces. He thought it wise that they proceed with caution especially considering who Two Dogs was and who he had been in the past. Still, the warriors' approach didn't impress him.

Morning Bird stopped still several feet from Two Dogs while Meniish flanked Delbert.

Morning Bird eyed Two Dogs.

"Why did you wave?"

Two Dogs dismounted his horse; he was growing tired of the warriors. Two Dogs thought if he were still leading warriors, he would have handled the situation more cautiously and far more aggressively. He learned that instilling fear in the hearts of a possible threat often quelled a problem before it started.

"Look, the Ghost we are hunting has veered south; he is making ground to your summer camp."

Morning Bird examined the hoof prints. Two Dogs spoke the truth. Morning Bird's eyes widened; Mason and Gabriella were alone, and neither could know that a killer was riding towards them.

"Meniish, Two Dogs speaks the truth. Go quickly, get the warriors, and ride hard to the summer camp."

Meniish nodded before bolting back towards the Clan.

Morning Bird kicked his horse, sending it full gallop towards the meadow, followed closely by Two Dogs and Delbert.

Mason and Gabriella

Mason woke, rolling onto his left side; he smiled as he watched Gabriella gently stroking their six-month-old baby boy Nyemii's head.

Mason could think of nothing better than waking to the sight of Gabriella and Nyemii. Nyemii kicked his chubby legs cooing at Gabriella. He was content and unaware of anything other than the comfort of his mother and father, who lay on either side of him.

Mason had protested naming his son Mason, not because he disliked his name but because he felt it would confuse the Clan when they said Mason. Would they be referring to him or his son? But Gabriella would not have it any other way.

In the end, a compromise was made between Mason and Gabriella. Their son's English name would be Mason, but he would also be known by his Kumeyaay name, Nyemii, and so he had two names, Nyemii Hill and Mason Hill Jr.

Gabriella smiled at Mason, "Our son is like you, Mason. He is always hungry."

Mason grinned at Gabriella, his love and the reason he lived. Although culturally different, Gabriella's family accepted Mason into their Kumeyaay clan, and he was treated no differently than anyone else.

Mason grinned. "He's also like you; he wakes up too early."

Gabriella stroked Mason's cheek, "I get up early to make sure my men are taken care of. Without me, you both would not know what to do."

Mason rolled onto his back, glancing at the roof of their ewaa. It had been built well, lasted through the winter without leaking, and kept his little family warm through many cold nights. He had worried that their tiny home would not provide enough warmth. Still, he realized the ewaa was a shelter built by the Kumeyaay for over a thousand years. If constructed properly, an ewaa kept the elements at bay and provided a snug home.

Gabriella and Mason were alone. The Clan, as they had since the beginning of time, had returned to the desert in the fall. But, unfortunately, the gunshot wound that nearly killed Mason had rendered him unfit for the travel. So it was decided among the Clan and primarily upon Gabriella's insistence that Mason winter over in the Clan's Summer camp until he fully recovered, and so it was.

So as not to leave Mason, Gabriella, and Nyemii alone for longer than needed, an agreement had been made among the Clan that they would return much earlier than they usually would. A decision that greatly excited Gabriella's mother.

Fortunately, It had been a relatively easy winter; However, Gabriella had insisted that Mason was not well enough to travel. He still could do day-to-day chores, which usually included doing menial tasks assigned by Gabriella, and there was always a never-ending list of menial projects.

Gabriella felt that Mason had to keep moving, he needed exercise to heal his shoulder and rebuild his muscle, so she kept him busy performing every chore she could think of.

Mason watched as Gabriella gently lifted their son from his little nest of fur blankets.

Gabriella gently placed Nyemii to her breast, humming a Kuymeyaay lullaby while feeding her precious son.

Gabriella grinned at Mason, "Don't worry, husband, I will make your food when he is finished."

Mason reached up and stroked Gabriella's cheek.

"I'm not worried, my love; you and Nyemii come before anything else."

Gabriella leaned forward, kissing Mason's forehead.

"I know, husband, and now that you have to wait, you can get some kindling for me."

Mason smiled. "Gabriella, I don't think you're happy unless you have me working on something."

Mason had no idea how true that was.

"I am happy you are alive to do things for me, husband. You almost died. Work is good for you. It will keep you strong. I need you to be here until we are old."

Mason grimaced as he pulled his blankets back and stood.

"Gabriella, I will be with you when we are old and in the next life."

Gabriella noticed Mason grimace as he stood. The gunshot wound that nearly took his life still had not completely healed. She knew Mason was not telling her how much it still hurt him, but she was determined to get him back into shape.

Mason ducked through the door of the ewaa and into the cool morning air. He paused to stretch and look around the green, peaceful meadow where he and Gabriella had lived alone for many months.

The sun had just begun to cast its light on the tallest pines, and the sweet smell of the lush green grasses lining the stream filled the air.

Before walking to the nearby oak trees for kindling, Mason glanced over his shoulder at his tiny home. He couldn't imagine a better life other than the one he was living. Mason had everything he always wanted. He had a beautiful wife, a child, and a family who loved him.

There were times when Mason would think of his mother. He missed her and his old dog. He also missed his father, who had been wrongly hanged, leaving his mom to raise him and run their ranch.

Although losing his father at a young age was terrible, Mason's mother ensured she provided everything she could for him.

If it hadn't been for the corrupt Sheriff assaulting his mother, Mason would have never been forced to run from the only life he knew; but that's what happens when you gun down the Sheriff of a small town.

It didn't matter to the Law that the entire town backed Mason's reasoning for gunning down the Sheriff. All the Law was concerned with was that an elected Sheriff had been killed. Eager to bring swift justice, the U.S. Marshalls Office dispatched Delbert, Tommy, Levi, and Two Dogs. Capture was expected within a month. Yet, a year later, the Marshalls still hadn't captured Mason.

Fortunately for Mason, the newly elected Governor of Colorado reviewed his case and issued a full pardon during his time on the run.

Mason was a firm believer that everything happens for a reason. He rationalized that what happened was destiny. If it hadn't happened, he would never have had to go on the run, and he would never have met Gabriella, who loved him and gave him a son; but still, Mason missed his mother and planned to visit her someday. He wanted her to meet Gabriella and her grandson. He also wanted her to see that he was happy and well.

Those plans were nearly destroyed six months earlier when Mason took a bullet in the back fired from the rifle of a ruthless Bounty Hunter named Dale Thorpe.

When he woke from his coma, Gabriella told him about Marshall Crenshaw and Two Dogs arriving for no reason other than telling him he had been pardoned. She also told him about the two Bounty Hunters who had hunted him and how they had met their deaths at the hands of the Kumeyaay women.

Now that he was no longer wanted, Mason felt he could live a normal life, which he intended to do. He held no animosity toward Two Dogs and Marshall Crenshaw. As he saw it, they were just doing their jobs.

Mason was fortunate that the Bounty Hunter's bullet had not killed him, and now, other than the nagging pain in his right shoulder and occasional numbness in his right hand, he felt back to normal. Mason figured a little discomfort was far better than being dead. Fortunately, Gabriella had nursed him back to health and bore him a perfect son, giving him more reason to be grateful to be alive; he felt truly blessed.

When Mason returned to the warmth of his and Gabriella's ewaa, he neatly stacked the firewood beside Gabriella's cooking fire.

Gabriella finished feeding Nyemii, tucked him snuggly back into bed, and prepared the morning wiiwish.

Mason sat beside Gabriella and watched as she hummed a pretty melody while she mixed acorn flour and dried berries for breakfast.

Gabriella glanced at Mason. "Mason, our family will be here any day. They will be happy to see you are so well."

"Your mother will be happy to see Nyemii; I feel sorry for the boy. He's going to be kissed and squeezed nonstop." Mason thought for a moment, "Gabriella, what name are you going to have the Clan call Nyemii?"

Gabriella shrugged as she put wood on her cooking fire.

"I will tell them to call him Mason. I chose that name; you chose Nyemii."

"Gabriella, are you upset that I call our son Nyemii?"

Gabriella placed her cooking olla in the small fire and leaned toward Mason, gently kissing his lips.

"No, Mason, he is our son; even with no name, I would not be upset."

Mason grinned, "I guess I should have called him no name then."

Knowing his teasing would rile Gabriella, he quickly turned to dash out the door, but Gabriella was too quick. Before he could escape, she playfully picked up a small branch and swatted his backside.

"Stop with your jokes Mason. You will eat your food; we have to bathe before you start working on the roof."

Mason's brow furrowed, "The roof? There's nothing wrong with it."

As Gabriella poured two bowls of wiiwish, she shrugged.

"That is why you need to work on it. It does not leak but could if you don't work on it."

Mason knew better than to argue with Gabriella. So instead, he took both bowls and walked with Gabriella to the rock, where they ate breakfast every morning.

Mason put his arm around Gabriella as he sipped his breakfast and looked across the expanse of their meadow.

* * *

Once Mason and Gabriella finished breakfast, Gabriella returned to the ewaa to get Nyemii for the family's morning bath.

As Mason walked hand in hand with Gabriella to the stream, he thought of the cold water awaiting him. He still hadn't gotten used to their frigid morning baths, but it was a custom that Gabriella would not allow him to skip.

As they stripped their clothes and entered the stream, little Nyemii seemed to understand what he was in store for. He kicked his chubby legs and cried in protest as Gabriella washed him in the frigid water.

"He fusses like you, Mason, this is done every morning, and he still fusses like you." Gabriella softly hummed as she washed Nyemii's hair. "He is my fussy Mason."

"He fusses because it's cold."

Gabriella rolled her eyes, "Mason clean yourself; you have things to do."

Mason splashed in the stream, quickly bathing himself, as Gabriella watched him laughing.

"I like to see you with no clothes, Mason."

Mason grinned before kissing Gabriella's forehead and quickly stepped out of the stream.

"I like seeing you with no clothes too, but it's much better when we're in bed."

Gabriella smiled shyly. "Later, Mason, you need to fix the roof."

Mason took Nyemii from Gabriella's outstretched arms while she finished bathing. Mason looked into the eyes of his son. Nyemii's eyes were his mother's, and his nose and the shape of his face were his.

To Mason, no child was more beautiful than Nyemii.

After their morning bath, Gabriella swaddled Nyemii to her bosom. At the same time, she crushed yucca root, using the foaming sap as soap for her little family's clothes.

While Mason busied himself thatching the roof that didn't require repair, he glanced at Gabriella and Nyemii. They were content and entirely at home in their meadow, and so was Mason; when the time was right, Mason decided he would ask Gabriella if she would be willing to stay year-round in the summer camp.

Living in the desert every winter didn't appeal to him. He often wondered why the Kumeyaay migrated to the harsh desert during winter. Of course, the winter months wouldn't be as cold as in the mountains, but in Mason's opinion, it was far more beautiful than the desert.

That night, Mason played with Nyemii while Gabriella prepared a rabbit and wild onion supper. These were the times that Mason looked forward to the most. His family was safe in their ewaa, and after dinner, they would lay together in bed and discuss the many chores Gabriella had lined up for Mason.

Gabriella glanced from her cooking olla toward Mason and Nyemii.

"Mason, I think our family will be here tomorrow. The air feels different."

Gabriella often sensed things that inevitably came to pass. It was a mysterious gift that Mason had learned was very accurate.

"If they'll be here tomorrow, that means they're close."

Gabriella laughed, "Husband, you say things that make me smile. Yes, that means they are close. If they weren't, then they would not be here tomorrow."

Mason realized how foolish his comment sounded. "I don't know why I said that." Mason grinned, "Gabriella, you make me smile with the things you say."

Gabriella grinned as she ladled their soup into bowls.

"Husband, how do I make you smile with my words?"

Mason patted the mat beside him and Nyemii.

"You make me smile because I love you, and sometimes you say things I don't understand."

Gabriella sat beside Mason, kissing him on the cheek.

"Husband, put wood on the fire before you eat."

Mason handed Gabriella his bowl laughing.

"And that is why you make me smile with your words. I'll put wood on the fire."

* * *

That night, Mason and Gabriella tucked Nyemii into his little spot in bed before sitting together beside the small fire and talking about the day's events and what the next day would bring when the Clan arrived.

The Beast Awakens

Ervin woke early to scrub jays cawing above him in the trees. He stared up at them from his temporary bed and watched as they hopped from branch to branch and curiously spied on the intruder.

Ervin grinned as he slowly reached for his rifle. His lust for killing wasn't limited to humans. Anything alive was fair game, and the peaceful Jays above him seemed to him as if begging him to take their lives.

Sensing the monster's intentions, the Jays scattered before Ervin could position his rifle to fire.

Ervin laughed, "Fly away, little birds."

The vision of the birds scattering triggered a long-ago memory. When Ervin was eleven, his mother asked him to kill one of their chickens for dinner. That was the first time she asked him to kill one of their hens, and when he realized how much he enjoyed killing a living creature.

Ervin remembered the chicken running to him, expecting to be fed. Only to be snatched up and whisked to the chopping block. He clearly remembered every moment of the act. From the hen's futile thrashing to escape to the moment he dropped the ax, severing its head and sending it into a spasm of dying reflex.

That day, Ervin felt a sense of fulfillment he had never experienced before; but the exhilaration of the kill was short-lived, and coming down from his murderous high was miserable.

Two days after the chicken beheading, Ervin walked his old dog to the creek behind his house. As he had all his life, the old hound remained loyal at his side, even as Ervin removed one of his mother's butcher knives from his waistband. He recalled the confused look in his faithful friend's eyes as he thrust the knife into his throat, followed by a frenzied flurry of stabbing.

Unfortunately, the thrill of killing animals was short-lived. Ervin needed more, something more potent to satisfy his morbid addition.

A week later, Ervin spotted a small boy playing at the creek near his house on his way home from school. Ervin's desire to kill the boy was overwhelming, and the situation was perfect.

Ervin didn't recognize the boy; this was an added bonus to the scenario. Not recognizing him meant the boy was probably from out of town and was likely visiting family or passing through. Ervin thought that not knowing the boy would make it easier to kill him.

The boy was alone and far enough out of town that no one would hear his screams. Everything was lining up as it should.

Ervin glanced up and down the dirt road; he saw no other children or adults. Ervin picked his way down the bramble-lined creek to where the boy was barefoot and splashing in the water.

Ervin sized up his victim, formulating a plan of attack. The boy was small and no older than eight, while Ervin was eleven years old and tall for his age. Ervin had the advantage in height and weight. The boy didn't stand a chance.

Noticing Ervin, the little boy stopped his splashing and smiled.

"Hey, do you want to play pirates with me?"

Ervin grinned as he sat and took off his shoes.

"Sure, I don't have nothin to do at home today so ma won't miss me for a little while."

The little boy reached down, cupping a handful of water, and splashed Ervin.

"I'll be the Captain, and you can be my first mate. That's what all the pirate stories say. There is a Captain and a first mate."

Although the little boy's splash infuriated Ervin, he smiled.

"That sounds fun, Captain."

Ervin waded into the creek, pretending to be interested in something submerged at his feet.

The little boy stepped beside him.

"What do you see?"

Ervin pointed. "Look close; I think I see gold."

Ervin picked up a fist-sized rock as the little boy bent low, searching the water.

"Where? I don't see any-"

Ervin slammed the rock into the back of the little boy's head, sending him head first and lifeless into the water. Then, for good measure, Ervin held the little boy's bleeding head underwater for several minutes before releasing his dead body to the current.

Ervin quickly put his shoes on and ran home. He had never felt more exhilarated in all his life.

So It had begun; the beast had awoken.

* * *

Ervin sat up; he surveyed his surroundings, spotting a faint impression of a trail leading south. Ervin decided that would be the path he followed for no other reason than it was leading in the direction he was traveling.

Unknown to Ervin, the trail led to a peaceful meadow occupied by a single man, his wife, and their baby.

Evil Lurks

Ervin followed the path south for a mile through the forest before the trees opened to a beautiful lush meadow. Ervin stopped, deeply inhaling the crisp pine-scented air, which he realized was also mixed with the faint scent of smoke.

With predator pinpoint vision, Ervin spotted a small ewaa in the distance. Smoke wisped and tangled from the smoke hole in the center of the tiny home's roof, confirming it was occupied. Then, to his great pleasure, he spotted a nude woman cradling an infant as she waded through the cattails and into a stream.

Ervin scanned the surrounding area for the woman's husband but saw nothing; still erring on the side of caution, he veered east into the tree line.

Erving halted his horse in the dark shadows of the forest and watched the woman as she lovingly bathed her child. Ervin knew immediately that he would kill both of them. However, he hadn't yet decided which one would die first when a man stepped out of the ewaa.

Ervin was surprised to see he was a white man. Ervin watched as the man stripped his clothing and waded into the stream with the Indian woman and baby.

The couple laughed as they bathed together, leaving no doubt in Ervin's mind that they were husband and wife. That called for a change in plans.

A man living deep in the woods was likely hiding from the law, which meant he might be good with a gun, and too wise to fall for any stories Ervin could think of. Or he was simply a mountain man who chose a life away from civilization, which also meant he was probably good with a gun and extremely wary of strangers.

In either case, Ervin resolved that he would have to kill the man first so he could take his time with the woman and baby; and so he formulated a plan. First, he would wait for the woman to wander away from her home, then drag her and her infant into the forest and kill them. If that plan didn't pan out, he would wait for the man to leave, then swoop in for the kill. Either way, he wasn't leaving until he satisfied his addiction.

* * *

Ervin spent his day watching the man work on the roof of his home. While his wife washed clothes and tended to her domestic chores. He grew agitated as he wasted his day watching the family. The woman and her child were his fix, and they were flaunting it in his face.

As the day began to fade into evening, Ervin resigned himself to the fact that he would have to wait until the following morning to make his move.

Ervin retreated deeper into the cover of the forest where he slept. His dreams were filled with bloody fantasies, which lulled him deeper into blissful sleep.

Flight of the Ghost

Morning Bird arrived at the meadow early the following morning, accompanied by Two Dogs and Delbert. Minutes later, the rest of Morning Birds warriors arrived.

The ten warriors, including Two Dogs and Delbert, lined side by side to one another on a hill at the north end of the meadow. None of the men spoke; instead, they scanned the dimly lit meadow. Mason and Gabriella's ewaa appeared to be secure. Nothing indicated that anything had happened out of the ordinary.

Morning Bird signed to his warriors, telling half of them to flank to the east side of the meadow while the rest were to follow him to Mason and Gabriella's ewaa.

While Morning Bird and his Warriors began their search, Delbert and Two Dogs rode directly south, straight through the center of the meadow.

Morning Bird and his five warriors silently rode to the ewaa before dismounting. As Morning Bird approached the ewaa, he fitted his bow with an arrow. His warriors followed suit, surrounding the ewaa.

With his warriors in place, Morning Bird deeply inhaled before bursting through the door.

Gabriella screamed as she pulled Nyemii to her chest. At the same time, Mason sat up with his colt pointed directly in the center of Morning Bird's face.

"Morning Bird, what in the hell are you doing?" Yelled Mason as he lowered his gun. "I damn near blew your head off."

Wide-eyed and aware of how close he came to traveling to the afterlife, Morning Bird lowered his bow.

"Mason, I am pleased to find you and Gabriella safe. I am here with Two Dogs and Marshall Delbert. They are hunting a man who they say is a killer. His tracks lead here."

Mason yanked his covers aside, grabbing his rifle. "Did you find the man?"

Morning Bird glanced over his shoulder.

"No, Two Dogs will track him. They say this man has killed many. It will not be safe here until we find him."

Mason glanced at Gabriella and Nyemii.

"I'm staying here with my wife and son."

"Yes, you will. Meniish and the other warriors are here; they are spreading through the meadow. We will find this man."

Gabriella touched Mason's shoulder.

"Mason, give me your knife. I will kill this man if he comes."

The Clan knew Gabriella as a woman warrior. Since childhood, she had proven herself every bit as fierce as the best of warriors. A fact that Mason had briefly forgotten.

Mason glanced at his knife before looking into Gabriella's eyes. The softness of her almond-shaped eyes had been replaced with fiery anger.

"Mason, I will not ask again; give me the knife."

Mason did as he was told; he was reminded that Gabriella had a warrior's heart that couldn't be tamed by motherhood or marriage. He wasn't about to test her.

Gabriella tucked Nyemii into his spot before positioning herself near the door of the ewaa.

"Morning Bird, leave us. Find this man."

Morning Bird nodded; although Gabriella was not a warrior leader, she was respected by all of them. During their childhood together, Gabriella had beaten all of them for minor infractions.

A fact that had never been forgotten by any of them.

As Morning Bird and his warriors mounted their horses, Morning Bird signed to the warriors, searching the east that Mason and Gabriella were alive.

* * *

Delbert and Two Dogs were relieved to see Mason followed by Gabriella, step out of their ewaa.

Two Dogs waved before heading east toward the treeline.

"The Ghost will be hiding. If he saw Mason and his wife, he did not spare them out of sympathy. He spared them because he is waiting for the right time to kill them."

Two Dogs scoured the woods, searching for Ervin's tracks as the warriors spread across the meadow.

Closing in

Ervin woke before sunrise. He felt like a child on Christmas morning, and the little family would be the gift he always wanted.

When Ervin arrived at the edge of the treeline, he spotted the warriors. They were fanning out on both sides of the meadow, and to his horror, the legendary Marshall Crenshaw and Two Dogs were riding in his direction.

Ervin turned his horse, sending it full gallop through the forest and as far away from the meadow as possible.

* * *

Within an hour, Ervin found himself riding downhill alongside a stream. Although it was risky, he decided to follow a small trail down the mountain. Following the trail would allow him to travel faster but make his path easier for the Lawmen to find.

Ervin had a sudden feeling of doom overcome him. Two Dogs' tracking skills were legendary and spoke of in the criminal underground. It was well-known that once Two Dogs picked up a man's scent, there was no hope of shaking him.

Ervin grit his teeth; everything was going according to plan. He didn't have a care in the world as he traveled towards his new hunting grounds deep into Mexican territory, but that was over. He was angry with himself for taking his time during his journey. In hindsight, he should have assumed he was actively being tracked. Now he would have to keep an eye on what was behind and in front of him.

* * *

Two Dogs found where Ervin had sat to watch his prey and later the spot where he had slept.

Morning Bird and Meniish rode with Delbert and Two Dogs, not letting them out of their sight.

Two Dogs turned, facing Morning Bird and Meniish.

"The Ghost slept here before going to the tree line. He must have seen us and fled south. Morning Bird, you are your warriors' leader. You decide what course to take. Follow us or return to your summer camp and make it safe for your Clan's arrival."

Morning Bird thought for a moment. He knew there was no need to continue following Delbert and Two Dogs. They were not a threat.

"Meniish, these are white man problems. Our people are our concern. We will do as Two Dog has suggested. We will turn every rock in the meadow and make it safe for our people."

Meniish agreed, "The Clan will be here when the sun is high. I should take four warriors with me back to them so they know they are safe."

As his second in command, Morning Bird agreed with Meniish.

"Go to them; the rest of us will prepare." Morning Bird directed his attention toward Two Dogs and Delbert. "Leave here, and know that you are not enemies of the Kumeyaay. Find this Ghost or killer, or whatever it is you call him."

* * *

Mason and Gabriella watched the warriors as they scoured the surrounding forest. Mason felt a pang of regret that he couldn't ride with the men and hunt down the killer who had dared to wander onto their summer camp. But he knew his place was with Gabriella and Nyemii. If need be, he would protect his family to the death.

Gabriella spotted Morning Bird and Meniish as they rode along the easterly tree line.

"Mason, look." Gabriella pointed toward the two warriors. "They have come back alone."

Mason squinted, scanning the vast meadow until he spotted the two warriors.

"That's a good thing, Gabriella; that means the killer Two Dogs and Marshall Crenshaw are tracking is gone."

Gabriella reached for Mason's hand.

"Husband, I have never felt unsafe here before. There have never been problems. Now all of this. It was the manhunters who tried to kill you, then the Lawmen came, not one time but now two times. I do not like this."

Mason tenderly kissed Gabriella's forehead. He knew he was the reason outsiders intruded on the Clan's otherwise peaceful existence.

"Gabriella, we're safe; the Clan is here, and whoever Two Dogs and Marshall Crenshaw are tracking is gone."

Gabriella handed Mason his knife.

"I need to feed our son; you go to Morning Dove and see what he has to tell."

Gabriella turned to enter the ewaa but not before glancing over her shoulder at Mason.

"I love you, husband."

Mason grinned as he did every time Gabriella told him she loved him.

"I love you, wife."

As Mason walked toward Morning Bird and Miniish, his heart grew heavy. As much as he wanted to stay in the meadow year around, he had Gabriella and Nyemii to care for, and their safety came first. If he were alone, he wouldn't have worried about intrusion or men who may come to harm him. Mason was confident in his handling of a gun. Although he had never killed for any other reason than self-defense, a handful of grave markers stood as monuments to those he had felled.

Mason crossed the stream, meeting with Morning Bird and Meniish.

"I assume Marshall Crenshaw and Two Dogs picked up the trail of the man their hunting."

Morning Bird nodded. "They did; this man they are looking for is not our problem. He has left, and no one was harmed. He is the white man's problem."

Mason glanced toward his ewaa. "If he comes back this way, I'll kill him myself."

"You will not kill him yourself." Morning Bird chuckled. "If the man returns, we will capture him and let the women kill him. Their methods are slow and will cause great pain."

Mason whistled. "Gabriella told me what the women did to the men who tried killing me. He better think twice before coming back."

Morning Bird nudged his horse forward. "Mason, the warriors are clearing the meadow. The Clan will be here soon; you should go to Gabriella and your son. Make your ewaa ready for Manuel and Isabel Morning bird grinned. "Mason, I feel for you; Isabel will scold you no matter how good of a father you are."

Mason understood exactly what Morning Bird was referring to. Mason loved his mother-in-law, but she was quick to reprimand him if she thought her grandson wasn't completely spoiled. Mason learned that lesson shortly after Nyemii was born. Isabel constantly watched him. If she didn't think Mason was holding Nyemii properly, she would take him and show Mason how to hold a baby. If Mason cleaned Nyemii, she would nudge him aside and scold him for not cleaning his son correctly.

Mason understood that Isabel was an overly protective grandmother. Still, there were times when he had to grit his teeth not to say something he would regret.

Meniish playfully shooed Mason toward his ewaa. "Go, Mason, make your bed away from Gabriella and Nyemii. Your mother-in-law will be sleeping in your spot tonight."

Mason knew Meniish's joke was probably true. Isabel would undoubtedly want to sleep beside her grandson and Gabriella, while he would be forced to sleep beside his father-in-law, Manuel. He took solace in knowing that would only be for a single night. He vowed to help Manuel build his ewaa as quickly as possible.

"Morning Bird, make sure to tell everyone to call Nyemii by the name Gabriella gave him. Nyemii is what I call my son; Gabriella wants the Clan to call him Mason."

Morning Bird and Meniish shook their heads, they couldn't understand why Gabriella insisted on naming her son the same as her husband, but it wasn't a topic either of them dared to question.

"We will tell everyone; we would not want to see Gabriella force you from your ewaa." Both warriors laughed, but they knew it could be a real possibility.

Mason grinned, "Thank you, brothers; I better get me and Manuel's bed ready."

As Mason returned to his ewaa, he heard Morning Bird and Meniish laughing behind him; he smiled; he was happy that his family had returned.

Death Sentence

Two Dogs quickly found Ervin's tracks leading down the mountain's southern side, and it was evident that Ervin was moving swiftly.

Two Dogs briefly halted his horse, scanning his surroundings.

"Delbert the Ghost is very close. He is heading south."

"So he's back on track to Mexico?"

Two Dogs shrugged. "It looks that way, and he is moving fast. It would be best to take him in the open desert. There are too many places to seek cover in the forest."

Delbert nodded; capturing a desperate man in the desert would be much easier, but that could be a double-edged sword. Minimal cover for a desperate man meant minimal cover for his pursuers.

Two Dogs nudged his horse forward, followed by Delbert.

"Dogs, I've been doing some thinking. I think we should execute Ervin, regardless of whether he surrenders."

Two Dogs smiled; Delbert's plan was not endorsed or within policy of the U.S. Marshall's apprehension policies, but considering Ervin's crimes, it was fitting.

"Delbert, I agree, but I think it would be wise that you never suggest such a thing with another Lawman."

"Dogs, there won't be another Lawman to discuss this with. I'll have no other partner but you. If they try partnering me up with someone else, I'll retire on the spot."

"Then we will kill the Ghost. Even if he surrenders."

The Reckoning

Ervin followed the trail to the desert floor. From the shade of the last tree, he scanned the vast open desert before him. The flat boulder-laden landscape became hilly two miles ahead with large rock outcroppings. Ervin knew it was now or never; he had to move quickly to avoid being caught in the open.

Ervin sent his horse full gallop towards the nearest outcropping of rocks. As he rode, he expected Two Dogs and Delbert to be closing behind him, which led him to push his horse harder. If he could reach the hill, he could take cover and, with luck, outsmart and kill the two Lawmen.

* * *

Delbert and Two Dogs reached the edge of the forest. In the distance, they saw a black speck trailed by a low-hanging cloud of dust.

Two Dogs grinned. "So there is the Ghost; he is riding hard."

"Dog's he's riding hard because he knows we are closing in. He's trying to make it across the flats to a place where he can hide."

As Delbert finished his sentence, Ervin rode up a small hill and disappeared into a cluster of boulders.

It was just past three, with hours of sunlight left. Two Dogs turned his horse back into the forest. "Delbert, we will rest in the shade until night. Then we will make our move."

126

Delbert followed Two Dogs; if they tried pursuing Ervin across the flats in broad daylight, Ervin could take his time picking them off from a safe place of cover.

But on the other hand, crossing the flats after dark would provide them with concealment.

Delbert and Two Dogs sat in the shadows of the trees, staring at the distant hill and temporary lair of Ervin.

Delbert absentmindedly chewed on a stem of dried grass.

"You know, Dogs, I think Ervin might try slipping away down the backside of that hill as soon as it's dark."

Two Dogs rested on his elbow, seemingly unconcerned whether or not Ervin fled in the night.

"It doesn't matter, Delbert. We are too close to lose him; by tomorrow, the Ghost will need to find a new body to possess."

Delbert stared at the desert landscape ahead. Although he didn't want to discuss Two Dogs story about Coyote, it bothered him. It was one thing for Two Dogs to recite superstitious beliefs but an entirely different thing to tell him he had actually seen something he believed was a spirit.

Delbert cleared his throat. "Dogs, you mentioned a while back that you saw Coyote and that he was following us."

Two Dogs rolled onto his back, staring into the canopy of trees.

"I did, and I told you that Coyote would not tell me why he was following. I feared he would cause us problems, but he hasn't."

127

"Maybe he changed his mind, Dogs. Maybe he decided following us wasn't worth his trouble."

Two Dogs shrugged. He had thought the same thing.

"Maybe, but I have never heard of a Spirit Walker revealing himself and not doing what it said it would do."

" I guess I don't understand how these things work. I'll be honest, Dogs, the whole thing doesn't make sense to me."

"Delbert, no one can predict what a Spirit Walker will do or why they do it. They do not think as we do."

Delbert resigned himself to the fact that the topic of Spirit Walkers would result in no real understanding of Two Dogs' spirit world beliefs.

Rather than ask any more questions, Delbert lied down. He wouldn't see Ervin at this distance even if Ervin stood on top of a boulder and waved his arms. His far-sightedness troubled him; it was yet another sign of his age catching up to him.

A year earlier, he could still see far into the distance; now, he relied on Two Dogs to spot any adversary more than two hundred yards away.

Nevertheless, he took solace in knowing he could still spot and outshoot anyone posing a threat at a reasonably close distance.

As Delbert strategized the night assault on Ervin, his mind fogged, ultimately rendering him asleep.

Two Dogs glanced at Delbert; his rhythmic breathing signaled that he was deep asleep. Two Dogs decided to let Delbert nap, the ride had been taxing, and blood would be spilled soon enough.

Two Dogs sat up and stared at the distant hill where he knew Ervin was hiding and planning his next move.

* * *

Ervin sat in the shade between two boulders. He stared at the distant tree line, expecting Two Dogs and Delbert to appear at any moment. When they didn't, he trained his eyes on where he had emerged from the forest and crossed the flats.

For over an hour, Ervin sat motionless, staring at the tree line. Then something tugged at his subconscious. He knew someone was staring back at him, patiently waiting for him to make a move.

Again Ervin cursed himself for being so careless. He had taken his time indulging his addiction, and now Lawmen were closing in, and not just any Lawmen; it was Two Dogs and Marshall Crenshaw.

Ervin glanced up; it was past noon. In a few hours, he would make a run for it; but he was suddenly aware that he had no idea where the next town was or where exactly he was running to. He also knew Two Dogs and Marshall Crenshaw didn't adhere to international borders or jurisdictions. He had heard a story about the two Lawmen hunting and capturing a man in the farthest reaches of Canada.

Ervin knew there was little hope in evading the Lawmen. The only way to stop them was to kill them, which was precisely what he had in mind. A life looking over his shoulder would be no life at all. He would never be free to kill whoever and whenever he wanted, and the thought of being the hunted and not the hunter didn't suit him.

As the hours passed, Ervin decided not to wait for nightfall. Doing so would not put any more space between him and the Lawmen. He had to make his move and make it now.

Ervin crawled back to his horse, which he had tethered on the hill's south side. As he mounted his horse, he scanned the distant southern terrain. The faint outline of mountains lay many miles away; if he could reach them, he figured he would have a better chance of shaking Delbert and Two Dogs. If he managed to kill them along the way, that would ensure that he would have a life of freedom.

Ervin nudged his horse forward so as not to kick up a trail of dust; he kept the horse moving slowly. How he saw it, a little distance was better than none.

* * *

Two Dogs watched the brilliant orange horizon of sunset. If not for the task at hand, he would have enjoyed the beginning of a warm night.

Two Dogs redirected his attention to the hill where Ervin had disappeared. The hill was quickly dissolving into darkness, and still, nothing moved. Then he saw them; a pack of eight coyotes was crisscrossing one another's path as they silently traveled across the flats and directly toward him and Delbert.

Two Dogs scanned the flats, searching for Coyote who he knew had to be nearby. As the coyotes trotted closer, the alpha male sniffed at the air; it had picked up the scent of Delbert and Two Dogs.

The alpha male stopped less than fifty yards from where Delbert and Two Dogs were hidden. Its keen eyes spotted the two Lawmen. The rest of the pack halted, waiting for the alpha to decide what to do next. Rather than go any closer, the alpha stood its ground, sniffing the air.

Two Dogs glanced past the alpha and his pack. Then, as if emerging from the sand, a man stood slowly to his feet. It was the Spirit Walker Coyote. Coyote signed to Two Dogs telling him Ervin was on the move and heading south.

Two Dogs stood before nudging Delbert with his foot.

Delbert awoke from a peaceful nap, shocked to see that the sun had set.

"Dogs, why didn't you wake me up sooner?"

Delbert scrambled to his feet, noticing Two Dogs locked stare toward the flats.

Delbert stepped to Two Dogs' side, scanning the open desert.

"What is it, Dogs? Is it Ervin?"

Before Two Dogs could respond, Coyote howled, calling for his pack to return to him.

"It is not the Ghost; it is Coyote. He says the Ghost is on the move heading south."

131

Delbert squinted his eyes, trying desperately to see Coyote. "Damnit, Dogs, I don't see anything."

When the pack reached Coyote, he turned and ran, leading his pack south and into the darkening desert.

"There is nothing to see, Delbert; Coyote is gone. We need to move quickly."

* * *

Ervin had ridden in darkness for several hours; he was beginning to think he may have somehow lost Two Dogs and Delbert. Or, at the very least, he was much farther away from them than he had thought he was. He toyed with the idea that the Lawmen may have never found his trail. Ervin knew that scenario was unlikely, but it wasn't out of the realm of possibility.

A mile ahead, Ervin saw the lights of a town and the porch lights of scattered ranches. He longed for a drink and a soft bed, but Ervin knew that was out of the question. Even a brief stop would attract attention, and information could be bought cheaply.

Instead, Ervin pressed on, eventually passing by the distant town. Ervin knew he had to come up with a plan. He had to kill Delbert and Two Dogs, but how?"

* * *

Even in darkness, Two Dogs was able to find Ervin's tracks.

"Delbert the Ghost is a fool; even when he knows he is being tracked, he travels in a straight line; he doesn't try to hide his tracks."

"He doesn't hide his tracks because he thinks he's untouchable."

"The Ghost is making bad decisions; his mind is becoming poisoned."

Delbert glanced at Two Dogs. "What do you mean poisoned?"

"The spirit is growing tired of the body. It wants to move on to another. If the Ghost is not killed, the spirit will poison the body. It will invite disease and make the mind make bad decisions. It will do anything to kill the body."

Delbert nodded; although he didn't believe a word Two Dogs had said, he knew Two Dogs did. Delbert interpreted Ervin's carelessness as simple arrogance combined with a false sense of invincibility.

"Well, Dogs, if it's a new body the spirit wants, then we should make arrangements to help it on its way."

Two Dogs laughed, Delbert's sense of humor often confused him, but in this case, he understood.

"Yes, Delbert, we will help the spirit."

Within three hours, Two Dogs spotted the lights of the same town Ervin had seen hours earlier.

"Delbert, there is a town west of us."

Delbert grinned; although his eyesight wasn't what it used to be, he still could see distant light in an otherwise dark landscape.

"I see the town Dogs. My eyes aren't that far gone."

Two Dogs closely examined Ervin's tracks.

"The Ghost did not go to the town; he is still riding south."

"Looks like there's still a glimmer of sanity left in that head of his. Only a lunatic would ride into town knowing the law was right behind him."

"It was a wise decision, but he is still hours ahead of us."

Delbert nodded. "That's better than a day or more ahead."

* * *

As the sun slowly rose in the east, Ervin heard the calls of coyotes. Ervin glanced over his shoulder, not in fear but rather curiosity. Nothing appeared out of the ordinary, just a stark desert landscape as far as he could see. Yet the coyotes' calls were unusually excited.

Ervin spotted a deep green circle of fescue, cattails, and several cottonwoods a half mile ahead. It was a lucky find; he needed to refill his canteens and water his horse. Plus, a brief break would allow him to stretch and relieve his backside from his saddle.

As Ervin rode closer, he spotted two horses tethered side by side to the stump of a willow. Several feet from the stump, two Mexican men were sleeping among the tall fescue.

Ervin grinned; he had found the solution to his problem.

Ervin stopped his horse and whistled. The two men immediately jumped to their feet, rifles in hand.

Ervin smiled as he raised his hands. He had to convince the two men; he was just a friendly traveler passing through.

"Friends, I'm only passing through. Do you mind if I water my horse?"

The shorter and much fatter man glanced nervously at his partner.

"Diego, who is that man?"

Diego grinned; although a seasoned criminal, he, like Ervin, acted as if he was a kind-hearted traveler.

"Forgive us, friend; of course, you can water your horse."

Ervin caught the split-second narrowing of Diego's eyes. He knew Diego was a dangerous man, and his partner was his dutiful yet simple-minded sidekick.

Ervin cautiously rode forward; dangerous or not, he was confident he could kill both men before they knew what hit them.

"Friends, my name is Earl; I was robbed by two men a few miles back."

Diego glanced at his partner. "Did you hear that, Luis? Earl was robbed."

Diego scratched his whiskered face; he didn't know what to think of this gringo. He spoke softly, but behind his smile, Diego sensed something evil.

Ervin decided now was the time to hatch his plan; beating around the bush would only give Diego time to study and possibly figure out that Ervin was a very evil man.

"Yup, they robbed me, taking three hundred dollars but not before tying me up."

Diego elbowed Luis. "Luis, the robbers took three hundred dollars." Diego shouldered his rifle. "So if these men tied you up and took three hundred dollars, how did you get away?"

Ervin raised his right hand, revealing his narrow wrists. "I have small wrists; I slipped away after they went to sleep."

Diego believed Ervin's story but wasn't sure where the conversation was going.

Ervin grinned; he knew his story was working.

"I have a proposition for you, gentlemen; I have fifty dollars left. I'll pay you to kill those men and get my three hundred dollars back."

Diego glanced at Luis; this stranger was a fool. He was willing to pay them fifty dollars to kill the men who had robbed him and expected them to return the money to him.

"Where are these men?"

Ervin thumbed over his shoulder, "They're not too far behind; I heard them say something about heading to a town south of here."

Luis blurted out, "Iron Wood, was it Iron Wood? It's south of here."

Ervin snapped his fingers. "That's the place, Iron Wood."

Diego's eyes narrowed; nothing in Iron Wood would interest travelers. It was a modest town with not much to offer. Its citizens were primarily cattle ranchers, and the few stores were filled with ranch and farm supplies.

"Friend, there is nothing in Iron Wood; why would these men be traveling there? And where are you going?"

Ervin reached into his pocket, pulling out a handkerchief containing fifty dollars in silver. Ervin tossed the handkerchief to Diego.

"My business has nothing to do with Iron Wood. I'm traveling farther south. " Ervin smirked. "Count the money; there's fifty dollars. As I said, the two men aren't far behind, and I want my three hundred. Kill them, and half is yours. When the job is done, I'll meet you in Iron Wood."

Ervin knew Diego and Luis were bandits; with fifty dollars paid in advance and three hundred more lining the pockets of two unsuspecting travelers, they couldn't resist; Diego pat Luis' shoulder. "I think Earl is lying; I don't think he has business anywhere. I think he is wanted and has come here to hide."

Ervin slid his hand slowly to the butt of his gun; things were beginning to unravel.

"But that doesn't matter." Diego winked at Ervin. "We'll kill both of them and get your money. You wait in Iron Wood. There is a cantina in town. Wait there; we will come."

Diego had no intention of returning Ervin's money. He would kill the two men, take their money and continue living a banditos life.

Ervin grinned; his plan was working out exactly how he had hoped. Ervin knew that even if his story had been true, the banditos would never settle for half the money. Or, for that matter, meet him in Iron Wood. It didn't matter; if he were lucky, the banditos would ambush and kill the Lawmen or at least slow them down.

Ervin nodded. "Thank you, gentlemen; I will see you in Iron Wood."

Ervin rode past the men before dismounting his horse and filling his canteens.

As Diego and Luis rode north to find their victims, Luis asked Diego.

"Are we really going to kill these men and bring the money to Iron Wood?"

Diego laughed. "No, Luis, what kind of fool do you think I am? We're going to kill the two men, take the money, their guns, horses, and anything else worth stealing."

Luis was relieved; he was convinced that Diego had lost his mind.

"So it's business as usual, Diego?"

"Yes, Luis, business as usual."

* * *

Two Dogs halted his horse when he spotted two riders approaching from the south.

"Trouble is coming, Delbert."

Delbert focused his attention south. "What kind of trouble?

"There are two riders; they are heading right at us."

"Maybe they're just heading north."

"No, Delbert, they are following the Ghost's tracks."

Delbert glanced at Two Dogs before returning his focus south.

"Why would they be following Ervin's tracks in the opposite direction? That doesn't make sense, Dogs."

Two Dogs shrugged, he wasn't sure why the riders were following Ervin's tracks, but he had a theory.

"Maybe these riders knew the Ghost; maybe they are coming to cause problems."

Delbert found it difficult to believe that Ervin had any friends, let alone two, that would do him any favors.

"So what's the plan, Dogs?"

"Delbert, I think we should keep going. If there is trouble, we will take care of it."

Two Dogs and Delbert unsheathed their rifles.

Delbert nodded. "Let's go."

* * *

When Diego spotted Delbert and Two Dogs riding toward him and Luis, he halted his horse.

"There they are, Luis, just like Earl said."

Luis grinned; this was going to be an easy heist. The two men wouldn't even know what hit them.

"How do you want to do this, Diego?"

Diego thought for a moment; the distance between them and the two riders would make shooting them off their horses difficult.

"I think we'll close the gap between them and us. When they get close enough, there will be no words. We'll shoot them before they have a chance to do anything."

Luis grinned; he was very familiar with Diego's cowardly tactics; it was a strategy they had used time and time again.

Neither of them was willing to get themselves in a gun battle. Robbery required the assailant to strike first, ensuring their safety and quickly dispatching their victims before anything could go wrong.

"I'll wait for you to give the word."

Diego unsheathed his rifle, followed by Luis.

"Just a little closer; I'll take the man on the left, and you take the one on the right. It will all be over quickly, and we'll be celebrating by nightfall."

Diego nudged his horse forward, followed by Luis. As they closed the distance between Delbert and Two Dogs, they slowly spread out from one another.

"You see what they're doing, Dogs? I think those two idiots are going to try robbing us."

Two Dogs nodded; he recognized the two men's tactical movements. They were fanning out from one another to make it difficult to mow them down with a single burst of gunfire.

"Delbert, I will take the tall one. Can you see enough to shoot the shorter one?"

Delbert tapped his rifle, ready for whatever came next.

"I see them just fine, Dogs; if this is how they want it, then that's how they're going to get it."

When Diego and Luis closed to twenty-five yards, Diego yelled. "Now!"

As Diego lifted his rifle from his lap, he felt a slap to his forehead before tumbling lifelessly to the ground.

Luis had only a moment to react when he felt a massive punch to his chest. He briefly stared into the sky as he fell backward in his saddle. The clouds above looked unusually beautiful before they faded into black.

Two Dogs glanced at Delbert. "Looks like they had a bad day Delbert."

Delbert placed the butt of his still-smoking rifle on his right thigh.

"Dogs, I would have to agree."

Delbert and Two Dogs cautiously approached the two dead men. Their life of crime had ended in the same manner as it had ended for many people who were unfortunate enough to have crossed their paths in the past.

Delbert noticed a handkerchief with its spilled silver lying beside Diego's crumpled body.

"Looks like they won't be spending that."

Two Dogs rode past the bodies undeterred. There was still work to be done, and as Lawmen, neither he nor Delbert intended to loot the dead men's bodies.

"It is probably stolen money; maybe someday someone passing through will find it and spend it on something worthy."

"I'd like to think so, Dogs, I really do." Delbert glanced at the dead men's fleeing horses. He didn't know if they were running in fear or exhilaration at finally being free of the bandidos. "Hopefully, their horses will find a decent home as well."

Delbert and Two Dogs continued south following Ervin's tracks, leaving the dead men and their confused horses behind."

Ervin rode past Iron Wood; from what he could see, it was just as Diego had described. There were a handful of run-down buildings and adobe houses scattered about, but no sign of a prosperous town. The citizens of Iron Wood were nothing more than poor cattle ranchers who would spend their entire lives trying to survive.

The thought of killing one or more of the miserable people crossed Ernin's mind. How he saw it, it would be a win-win situation. He could get his fix while putting some Iron Wood residents out of their misery.

But ultimately, he decided to move on. He had no idea if Diego and Luis had successfully killed his pursuers, and the gamble of assuming they had pulled it off was too great a cost.

As Ervin shielded his eyes from the desert sun, he scanned his surroundings. A rough road led from Iron Wood and twisted southward to god only knew where, but he knew every road had a beginning and an end. Ervin decided to follow it, staying well off its sporadically traveled course. He figured it had to lead somewhere and hoped that somewhere was a busy town where he could blend in and rest for a few days.

His dream of finding such a place came to a horrifying end when he glanced over his shoulder and spotted a thin cloud of dust north of him. Although he couldn't see the source, he knew there were two riders, and they had spotted him.

Two Dogs pointed south. "Delbert, there is a rider south of us. It is the Ghost. This will end soon."

Frustrated with his poor vision, Delbert grunted. "Dogs, if that is Ervin, this ends today. I want him dead, and I want him to know we killed him."

Two Dogs kicked his horse, sending it at full gallop, followed closely by Delbert.

Ervin glanced over his shoulder; he saw the two riders emerge like phantoms from the distant cloud of dust. He had been spotted, and the two Lawmen were racing towards him.

Ervin knew he had little chance of escape; his horse was old and unrested. Today would be the end of days for him or, as he hopelessly wished, the beginning of a new life free from his pursuers. All he had to do was find a place of concealment and pick them off like flies.

Ervin spurred his horse, forcing it to bolt toward a rocky hill a mile south.

Just as he made it to the base of the hill, a pack of coyotes, followed by the Apache warrior he had seen near Borrego, ran from an outcropping of boulders to his right, crossing directly in front of him. His horse reared in terror, throwing Ervin to the ground.

With the wind knocked out of him and dazed by the impact, Ervin struggled to his knees. His horse continued running uphill and into the concealment of the boulders ahead while the coyotes and the warrior continued east, howling as if they were pleased with what they had done.

Ervin glanced over his shoulder. The Lawmen were closing in; they were no longer featureless figures in the distance. He saw the look of determination on Delbert and Two Dogs faces.

Ervin picked up his rifle and stood on shaking legs. As he staggered up the hillside, he saw his horse standing at the top of the hill as if nothing had happened. If it weren't for the fact that he may still need her, Ervin would have shot her for leaving him behind.

As Ervin desperately sought cover from behind, he heard the distinct thumps of Lawmen's horses.

In desperation, Ervin spun, firing a single shot toward the advancing Lawmen before continuing his frantic flight.

Delbert instinctively ducked as Ervin's round hissed past his head, missing him by mere inches. Blind rage instantly overtook him; shooting a man in the back was against all moral and ethical codes, but at the moment, none of that made a difference.

Delbert stood in his stirrups, firing a single round into Ervin's left shoulder. Ervin momentarily crumbled before picking up his rifle and scrambling behind a cover of boulders.

Ervin felt the impact of the round, followed a split second later by the sound of a rifle blast behind him. He knew instantly that the Lawmen had no intention of bringing him in alive. It was going to be a fight to the death.

As he reached the relative safety of the boulders, he glanced at his horse. She was thirty yards from where he crouched. The irrational thought of running to her and fleeing briefly crossed his mind until a second gunshot was fired. This time striking his horse in the head. She was dead before she hit the ground.

Delbert jumped from his horse and scrambled to the cover of boulders right of Ervin's spot while Two Dogs sought cover to the left of his position.

Delbert looked toward Two Dogs mouthing, "Why?" He couldn't wrap his head around the fact that Two Dogs had shot the horse.

Two Dogs frowned before shrugging his shoulders.

Delbert would have laughed if they had been in any other situation, but now wasn't the time.

145

As the hours passed, all three men found themselves in a stalemate. Every time Delbert or Two Dogs tried to break cover and advance, Ervin fired from his sniper's nest. Although a terrible shot, neither Delbert nor Two Dogs were willing to gamble on Ervin getting in a lucky shot.

Ervin winced as he positioned his rifle atop a blistering hot boulder. The slug of Delbert's single shot was mercilessly embedded in his shoulder and grated against bone and tendon, rendering his left arm useless.

Ervin knew there would likely be no escape before he bled to death or died in a hail of bullets delivered by Delbert and Two Dogs, but he was determined not to let them have the satisfaction of him surrendering.

Ervin wiped his sweating brow on his right shoulder before carefully peering down the sights of his rifle.

There was no sign of Delbert or Two Dogs. Only his dead horse, lying exactly where Two Dogs had shot it, gave testament that he underestimated the aging Lawmen.

Ervin turned, resting his back against his cover, a large sun-scorched boulder. He glanced upwards; the sun was high, and the meager shade a nearby twisted creosote bush provided wouldn't prevent him from scorching like pork belly in a frying pan. Already his tongue was swelling, and dehydration from blood loss, coupled with the intensity of the desert heat, was beginning to take its toll.

Ervin forced himself to aim once again toward his horse. One of his canteens lay several feet from where his horse had fallen, surrounded by glinting bullets, which he desperately needed. His second canteen was still fixed to his saddle, beckoning him to drink.

Ervin licked his dry, cracked lips; he thought it might be worth a shot. He considered a quick sprint down the hill. He figured he could use the boulders for cover and retrieve his canteens and ammunition before Delbert or Two Dogs saw him.

As if reading his mind, a shot rang out. His fallen canteen spun as a bullet tore through it, followed quickly by a second shot that pierced his second canteen, spilling its contents from a large hole and down the side of the dead horse.

Ervin slammed his back against the boulder; anger seethed in him like white-hot flames. He would find a way to kill Delbert and Two Dogs and do so slowly.

A memory surfaced of a long-ago killing; it briefly calmed Ervin as he imagined delivering an identical death to Delbert and Two Dogs.

He had befriended a young couple and their young son under the guise of being a traveling preacher. When he rode into their camp and explained he had wandered off course, they fed him and agreed to let him sleep in their camp for the night. Unfortunately, they hadn't realized they were under the spell of a silver-tongued killer.

The following morning, the shattered husband and father of the young boy knelt shirtless and beaten beside the smoldering bodies of his charred wife and son. Ervin tortured them both for the entire night, forcing the man to watch before slowly burning them to death.

Ervin ended the man's suffering, but not before pulling his head back and carving a large X into his forehead. Ervin found it amusing that the man didn't resist or fight. His soul had already left, leaving behind a shell of a man. Ervin spat in the man's face before splitting his skull in two with an ax and leaving the family's bodies to rot.

Ervin grinned; he would find a way out of this and torture and kill the Marshall and Two Dogs.

Two Dogs fired a second round, striking the canteen strapped to the dead horse.

Delbert decided to make a break toward Two Dogs position. Ervins shooting skills had proven to be less than impressive, and he doubted Ervin had enough left in him for even a lucky shot. Still, Delbert ducked as he ran to Two Dogs position.

Delbert dove headlong beside Two Dogs, kicking up dust and sand onto Two Dogs.

Two Dogs spat grit from his mouth before grinning at Delbert.

"I didn't know you could still do that."

Delbert didn't know he could still pull a maneuver off like that either, and he wasn't surprised by the sudden ache in his knees and back.

Still, Delbert acted as if he wasn't hurt.

"Dogs, did you have to shoot the canteens? We could have used those."

Two Dogs frowned, "Delbert, the Ghost drinks poison. We would die if we drank from his canteen. Nothing the Ghost touches is safe."

"Is that why you shot his horse?"

Two Dogs shrugged, "I killed the horse because the Ghost possessed it," Two Dogs hesitated, "I also killed it because I knew it would anger the Ghost. The Ghost is still part man. That's why he bled when you shot him. Angry men make foolish decisions, the ghost will make a foolish decision before sundown, and when he does, we will kill him."

Delbert smiled at his old friend, "Dogs, you're my best friend and the wisest man I know. I don't know how many years we have left before we're too old for this hunting of man business, but as long as I'm able, We'll ride the ride."

Two Dogs peered around the boulder, searching for Ervin.

"Delbert, we have many years left, but when we run out, we will spend our last days telling stories to the young who will think we make lies. Until then, you should flank right and hold. The Ghost is waiting to make his move."

Before leaving, Delbert glanced at Two Dogs, "What makes you so sure he hasn't climbed down the back side of that hill and headed south?"

"There is nowhere for him to go. He has no water, no horse, and a bullet in his shoulder. There is nothing but desert to the south. But, from the hill, he can see Iron Wood to the north. That is the only place he can go."

Delbert nodded; Two Dogs was right; no man could survive traveling through the desert without water, and no man, no matter how depraved, would wander into the vast endless sea of the desert when he was in the eyesight of a town.

Delbert crawled into position fifty yards to the west of Two Dogs. From Delbert's vantage point, he could see the western slope of the hill and the northern face. If Ervin considered circling Delbert and Two Dogs from the West, Delbert would see him.

Five hours had passed since Ervin had been shot and two hours since his canteens had been destroyed. Still, the sun appeared to have hardly moved.

Ervin squirmed like an ant under a magnifying glass. He glanced at his left shoulder. Blood still seeped from his wound, soaking his entire left side. He no longer sweat in the intense heat, and his vision blurred.

Ervin knew it was now or never; if he remained where he was, he would bleed out. He had no choice but to return to Iron Wood, hoping Delbert and Two Dogs had given up and left. Ervin stood clumsily to his feet; the time had come.

Ervin staggered from behind the boulder, firing his rifle aimlessly from his hip. He saw his rounds striking the boulders near his dead horse, he heard his wheezing breathing, he felt the sting of the sun on the back of his neck, and he saw Two Dogs calmly walk from behind a large boulder in front of him.

Ervin staggered to a stop and grinned, "Well, Two Dogs, looks like you're about to meet your maker."

Two Dogs smiled as he calmly shouldered his rifle.

Ervin pulled his trigger, and the rifle responded, not with a discharge of a bullet but with a sharp click. Stunned, Ervin glanced down at his rifle.

Delbert casually walked from his position, stopping ten yards to Ervin's right.

Ervin swayed as he glanced from Delbert to Two Dogs.

"Now listen, gentlemen, this isn't fair. I'm out of bullets."

Delbert spat, "Ervin, you've been out of bullets; you've been dropping the hammer on that empty rifle all the way down the hill. We would have killed you hours ago if we knew you were out of ammunition.

Ervin shrugged, "The heat must be getting to me, Marshall. I was sure I was firing." Ervin glanced at his feet and the scattered bullets spilling from his saddle. "I don't suppose there's much hope that you gentlemen would consider taking me back to town? Ervin nervously glanced from Two Dogs to Delbert. "After all, Marshall, you are a Lawman. You can't shoot a man down when he's not a threat."

Two Dogs nodded, "You will die here, and our job will be done. No one will know your story, only ours. You died shooting."

Ervin smirked at Two Dogs before turning towards Delbert.

"I wouldn't expect much from a filthy savage, but what do you say, Marshall? Have a little heart; get me back to town. I have five thousand dollars in the bank. If you get me there and walk away, it's all yours."

Delbert spat at Ervin's feet. "Ervin, you didn't show mercy to any of the people you killed; but I'm a fair man who believes in second chances. Let me think about it for a minute." Delbert tapped his chin. "Naw, you're going to die right where you stand, but I'll tell you what, I'm going to count to five. When I start, you get to picking up and loading as many rounds as you can into that rifle. If you're lucky, you might shoot one of us before we cut you down."

Ervin licked his cracked lips. With delusional confidence, he knew he could load and fire in five seconds, killing the Marshall and Two Dogs in the process.

"Alright, Marshall, you start counting, and I'll start shooting." Ervin winked at Two Dogs, "I'm going to start by killing you."

Without warning, Delbert counted, "One, two."

Ervin dropped to his knees frantically, fumbling for the scattered bullets.

Finally, after managing to jam a single round into the chamber, he heard Delbert.

"Five."

Ervin looked up from his rifle and directly into Two Dogs' eyes. His last earthly vision was of Two Dogs staring down the barrel of his rifle, followed by a burst of gun smoke.

Delbert lowered his rifle; like Two Dogs, he had fired a single shot into Ervin's chest, ending the serpent's life.

Delbert clicked his tongue, "Ole Ervin shouldn't have tried shooting his way out of this. Hell, he could have had a long drawn, out trial, during which he could have pulled off another escape."

Two Dogs kicked Ervin's rifle from his dead right hand, "We'll stick to that. We tried to get him to surrender, but he chose to shoot it out."

Two Dogs knelt beside Ervin, inspecting his dead half-closed eye

"The ghost is free again; evil never dies; it moves from person to person."

Delbert shrugged, "I suppose it does, but evil has been officially evicted from this pile of horse shit."

Two Dogs grinned. "I do not think we should bury the Ghost. I think we should leave his body to the animals."

Delbert agreed; Ervin didn't deserve to be buried; he deserved to be eaten by wild animals and have his bones scattered and bleached by the desert sun.

Two Dogs stood, with a final nudge, with his boot to the side of Ervin's face. Satisfied that Ervin was dead, Two Dogs grinned at Delbert.

"Let's get back home and see who we're hunting next."

"Yes sir, Two Dogs and Marshall Crenshaw off on another wild adventure," Delbert laughed, "Hopefully, it won't be our last."

Epilogue

Delbert and Two Dogs eventually made their way back to their homes, where each had a couple of months to consider retirement.

However, Delbert's thoughts of retirement were short-lived and ended when the Postman handed him a telegraph.

Delbert read the brief details of his new assignment. It ended with orders to contact Two Dogs immediately.

Delbert looked up at the Postman.

"Would you mind sending a telegraph to a friend of mine?"

Manufactured by Amazon.ca
Bolton, ON